How to Find a Flock: Stories

Chris Vola

Contents

Marked

Waking at night, he pissed in the empty water or beer bottles that always seemed to pile up an arm's length away from his bed, corralled there by some unseen, magnetic-like force. He pissed in them because he couldn't walk to the bathroom and turn on the seizure-prone light-slash-fan, he couldn't flush the abnormally loud toilet, and he couldn't risk looking at himself in the grime-covered mirror.

Sometimes the bottle's opening would be too narrow or he'd really have to go and he would leak piss onto the floor or the laptop that he left closed next to his bed. He never wiped the droplets. They looked like star patterns in a photograph negative.

In the morning he would roll over and study the piss constellations. And though they never could portend what luck – good or ill – might be loosed upon him during the day, they were always a reminder that somewhere in the confines of that shuttered plastic box, waiting in frozen slumber, were the shards of something that might be described as resembling a life: favorited images of juvenile domesticated mammals that (he'd read somewhere) were likely to induce feelings of empathy and narrow the breadth of attentional focus; Groupons offering Delicious Deals and More Sparkly & Sweet Surprises; minimalist Tumblrs and image macros that dissolved before his eyes into puddles of fictive ennui; a soon-to-be-terminated back-and-forth with drtybklyngrl, who claimed to have fellated several middle-of-the-road alt-country drummers and described herself as "intentionally blurry."

He needed to feel like he was having moments.

He tried to ignore the perma-blinking phone buried nearby under the covers – the voicemails from creditors using words like "delinquent" and "culpable," the texts from at least two insignificant others probably calling him much worse than that. The unshakable dread that no matter what he did, the sum of his destiny would amount to nothing more than an asterisk on a mostly blank screen, a screen that would stare back at him with the coldness of a sniper sizing up his next target.

He could think of worse ways to wake up, and often did.

Last Girlfriend

She stops watching South Park because, no joke, Cartman reminds her of this blue and red oval-shaped electric egg called an iGasm that she and the Ex bought during a post-finals excursion to the city last semester. Actually, the toy was a joke, a reasonably funny one, but she knows that for a joke to continue working, you need an audience that at least sort of gets the punchline, otherwise you just come off looking a little nuts and lonely. So she finishes her homework and watches a YouTube video about a six-year-old in West Virginia getting spray-tanned and fitted for fake teeth before a pageant. "I'm smiling on the inside," the little doll announces into the camera without a hint of mountain twang.

She walks to a copier store that also has internet access. The only other person besides the bored Arab dude who manages the dust-pale hulks of decades-old machinery is a septuagenarian transvestite with thick burgundy lipstick and matching eye shadow reading an article on a scruffy desktop monitor with the headline LARGEST MILITARY EXERCISES ON THE ISLAND that looks like a Bachelorette recap. She sits next to the transvestite at the other desktop, waits for Internet Explorer to boot. The transvestite doesn't look up, mumbles what sounds like Haitian-celebrity-personal-trainer-baby at a half-loaded image of a woman clutching an infant.

When she's logged into Facebook, she goes to work, a massive de-tagging spree, erasing her name from many images – her shotgunning hookah smoke into the Ex's mouth; the two of them in matching flannels while she pretended to yank out the Ex's chin stud; the Ex (in uncharacteristic but festival-quality Goth makeup) shaving the side of her head during their short-lived dubstep obsession. By the time her fingers start to carpal she's removed her name from 847 photos, all of which correspond to what her mother describes as a "transitional orientation experience." Before she logs off, she changes her profile picture to a professional headshot taken at prom a year and a half ago: shoulder-length blonde hair, red and white floral-print dress, seated coyly, tan legs facing the camera. Vacant eyes that didn't care where to look.

She feels the tranny scouring her screen.

"Your sister's cute, hon."

Back at the dorm, Kandi's gone for the night. A rush event or a lacrosse social or something equally vanilla. She hopes Kandi will have the courtesy to get plowed at a frat residence instead of on the bunk bed they share, though she knows it's not likely. What were the lyrics to the song her and the Ex had written about her? Kandi's not one for walks of sha-a-ame, just nights of it! She notices a plum-colored cardigan and a lacy black bra and thong poking out from the wreckage of Kandi's closet. She sniffs them. Sweetly opaque, what she used to smell like before the Ex instituted a no-deodorant policy. She strips, puts on the underwear and sweater, helps herself to a seldom-used Marc Jacobs miniskirt, and heads to the bathroom. Products in pastel cases with names like Dream Nude and Baby Lips line the sink. She gathers what she needs, applies clumsily and reapplies. Stares into the mirror and tries to remember if the creamed-on face staring back looks anything like the prom photo. The eyes aren't right. As she leans toward the glass to fix them, a ringtone she thought she has deleted echoes from somewhere and she stabs herself with the eyeliner pencil.

*

The reviews she read on Yelp lauded the bar's "killer happy hour" and "chill lounge vibe," with music ranging from "Katy Perry to 90s alternative" and "THE BEST GUACAMOLE EVER =)." But the more immediate reason she wants to go is because she heard they never check IDs. She gets in without being stopped and with minor eye-groping from the bouncer, weaves her way through the beer pong traffic in the front, around de-suited post-collegiate brosephs screaming at various sporting events on the wall of flatscreens, past pseudo-familiar eyes that instinctively leer at Kandi's skirt, the exposed bra. Two girls from her dorm are sitting at the bar, slurping Long Island Iced Teas and cackling at their phones. She shimmies up to the stool next to them. They realize who she is and both start texting, meth-quick. She orders a Jack and Diet and a shot of Jameson from the melt-jawed bartender in his mid-thirties who might have been attractive once. She downs both, orders the same. She's finishing her third round when the bartender, who's bought her the last two, says something like how does it feel to be the most sought after object in the vicinity in a practiced hipster brogue and she ignores him; her rheumy eyes focus on a beer pong game.

He's older, rolled-up Oxford shirt, a face like Rachel Maddow but with better bone structure. Her gawking must be blatant because the guy he's playing with says something to him and points and they laugh and she thinks he's blushing but it might just be a beer flush. She swivels around, embarrassed, and she's about to order another round when a voice behind her says "Uh, I've got this one," to the bartender, who shrugs and pours without looking up. "Maddow" sits on the vacant stool to her right and the two girls from her dorm stop texting, glare. The specifics of the conversation are patchy – he's twenty-two or twenty-three, getting his masters in something monetarily useless, works part-time the vegan smoothie place across the street (but he's not, like, that crunchy), and lives in the neighborhood a couple blocks away. Not that it really matters. She's just floating on pleasantly hazed-over snapshots. His green (or are they hazel?) eyes searching her face's periphery. The awkwardly cute brush of his hand against hers as he reaches for his drink and his subsequent awkward apology. The jealous silence burning to her left. Proper drinks, of course, give way to well tequila shots and she doesn't remember why she's giggling so hard but it must be unforced because when he asks in a roundabout way if she wants to go back to his place – he's got an eighth of a potent new indica strain he picked up earlier and he's DVR'd the latest South Park – she leans over and whispers "fuck yeah homie," prettily she thinks, into his cheek. He blushes again. She turns to the texting girls, blows them a kiss and their mouths drop like they've been tasered or maybe just voted off the island.

*

His weed is sick, insofar as it creates a foot race between her head and her stomach to see which will disengage from her body first. Right now, it's dead even. South Park is a blaze of indefinite colors and the components of the living room – a dusty bookshelf, generic Japanese woodblock print posters, something that might be an old frat paddle or a snowshoe – are in similar states of blur. She braces against him to avoid feeling like she's tumbling off a building or maybe just the couch they're sitting on and he grins, blushes, wraps his arm around her shoulder, squeezes. At some point there's a crash in the dark hallway and a squint-eyed roommate creature emerges and demands in so many croaks that they remove themselves to a fucking bedroom because the creature has to be up for a fucking conference call in two fucking hours, which means they must have been discussing something – loud and…passionate? – for a long time and she doesn't remember what it was and it doesn't matter because she's happy to have her head lowered on a surprisingly comfortable pillow in a dim room lit by Christmas lights that outline the ceiling. He slumps over a laptop at a nearby desk and she stares at the blue and orange Hindu elephant and vaguely Celtic tapestries that line the walls, a décor choice she'd normally describe as mid-2000s-poseur or post-post-modern-bro-out, but which now seem to be helping to ward off the hurricane pounding the base of her skull. An electronic remix of a George

Michael song sifts through the speakers at a reasonable volume and he lies next to her on the bed and they stare at the ceiling until the song changes to a dubstep remix of t.A.T.u's "All The Things She Said." He starts to stammer, apologizing for the playlist and she grabs his crotch, rough strokes over his jeans and he pulls her face into his mouth, the shock of chin stubble, whiskey tongue, tongues, her fingers fumbling with his zipper, cupping, plying at the black lace and the skirt and thong collapsing in one motion onto the Persian-ish rug as she arches away because she's forgotten that she hasn't shaved in weeks but he pulls her hips against his, mumbles stale heat against her neck, how tight she is and she grunts – how long has it been since prom? – and his tongue's in her mouth then on her neck and she can smell herself, his sweat, getting closer, her fingers down there, bucking, still coming as he pulls out and releases a meager spattering on the plaid comforter. He rolls over and she stares at the ceiling, panting. The pants give way to chuckles and then to flat-out laughter, and it's like she's laughing at a video because as the wetness between her legs dissipates she feels herself floating up with it until she's somewhere near the

11

Christmas lights laughing down at her pants-less scarecrow legs; at him giving her this shy, endearing glance; at her patting his stomach, saying, "Congrats dude, you probably just bagged your first switch-hitter;" at her wriggling – still more than a little tipsy – gathering the clothes on the floor, putting them on while he finds his jeans and takes out a notebook and pen from one of the pockets; at him (avoiding eye contact) asking, "How does this work, can I, uh, get your digits?" and scribbles a monosyllabic nickname, a phone number and what looks like his Twitter handle on a piece of ripped-out paper; at him handing it to her and her stuffing it into her bra, at her mumbling something contrived like see you around and him lurching up and remembering, "Hey I never got your numb–" but not finishing and slumping onto the bed because she's already gone.

*

"Pageants can paint her way to something else, like a jewelry line, a candy line, or even just painting her way to success," a woman deadpans on a YouTube clip echoing from somewhere in the room. As she wipes

12

makeup and a few flecks of caked spittle from her face, the phone on the bathroom counter beeps twice in quick succession: a friend request and a text message ringtone she thought she'd deleted. She looks at the clean face, her face, staring back in the mirror, smiles, and reaches for the phone.

Bodies

There's a mist hanging over the valley. Darker and heavier than the drizzle-gray sky, thickening around the bowels of the largest trees, obscuring the path. At least that's the way I want it to look, posted up a couple blocks from where a massive plastic chimney rises from an open manhole, pumping steam vapor above pedestrian areas and into the boughs of the pigeon-spooge park that lines one side of the avenue, where the vapor joins with cigarette smoke from three raisin-eyed brown-baggers seated at the base of a statue depicting the gout-riddled wife of a robber baron environmentalist. "Parks are an ideal convergence point for potential donors, especially right after the close of normal business hours," is the kind of shit that Robbie, regional coordinator at Community Crusades, Inc., likes to write in his emails. Like I haven't been temping for the dork for the past two years.

It's almost six and I've barely seen any other people on the street during the two-mile hike from where I parked my on-its-deathbed Honda Civic, lugging the binder containing stacks of same-sex marriage statistics or water quality data or whatever progressive cause I'm supposed to be championing today. If I was smart, I would have called the office this morning and told them I wouldn't be coming in. Robbie's kind of squeamish, all I would have had to say was that I had extra-gnarly cramps, maybe mention a non-specific, yeast-related condition and I'd be home, no questions. But it's too late for that now. I wipe some raindrops from the collar of my florescent polo, skim the contents of the first pamphlet on top of the pile – a nonprofit that sends backpacks to kids in a Serbian economic oppression zone (good thing I'm wearing my entire rainbow of awareness bracelets) – and wait for the human downpour.

Chances are you've seen me, or someone like me, leering at you from the most awkward center of the sidewalk. Young, seemingly energetic, possibly dreadlocked, clipboard in hand, happy to disrupt your solitude and assault your sensibilities. "Excuse me, sir?

Do you support a woman's right to choose?" "Miss, do you have a moment to talk about sustainable agriculture in South Sudan?" And if you're like most sane people, you don't have a moment. You'll avoid eye contact (or praise yourself for remembering shades), you'll plaster your phone to your skull like it's the only thing keeping it together, or you'll pretend you can't hear me over the Norwegian black metal bumping in your earbuds when you're really listening to shit that's so light they wouldn't play it in elevators. My favorites are the hoodied futures-of-America who find it acceptable – no, necessary – to explain that AIDS is great for population control, or to scream "god hates fags and clipboarders!" at a five-foot-two, 105-pounds-after-a-burrito size chick.

To me, you're all PIN numbers that haven't expired yet, bodies I can use if you're dumb enough to listen.

As I watch the light disappear, I take out a handful of complimentary highlighters – featuring the same sad multi-ethnic child's face – from my cargo pocket, adjust my non-threatening ponytail and side-swept bangs, run my fingers over the holes in my naked earlobe, and listen for the first sounds of movement from the cubicled pens that line both sides of the street, hovering over first-floor retail façades. I pull out the tips of pamphlets so they're easily accessible. The first off-the-clock worker exits a building, scowl illuminated in phone glow. The pace quickens in a matter of moments, as I have anticipated, becoming a hail storm of seasonally flesh-toned galoshes and laptops wrapped in plastic bags, enveloping me in the stink of happy hour salivation.

I do something uncommon, a rookie move. Maybe it's the stress from still being so far below my projected savings for this quarter, maybe I'm tired. Either way, I allow myself to be hypnotized by the rapid beat of transit. I press the binder to my chest, close my eyes for barely a few seconds. I take a breath, feel water droplets pooling on the crow's feet that the Park Ranger called my "smile lines."

I open my eyes. Two business-casual fucktards — one flicking a music player, one struggling to zip the man-purse at his hip — are bee-lining, oblivious, toward the awkward center of the sidewalk and me and their inevitable confluence.

I brace for the collision. The impact knocks me back a foot or two, highlighters scatter. The drops trickle and run down my face. I resist the urge to curse, remain sightless, allowing the sensation to engulf me. I flick out my tongue, taste the sting of sludgy precipitation.

"UhhwoopsyouOK?" Purse Boy asks. I brush the water away and he's scooping my crap off the pavement. He mumbles what sounds like "Lyme-disease-free-yoga," presses the pens into my hand and walks away fast. It's better that way. Pity talkers are the worst. It's like I get it, you feel bad that you bumped me, that it's cold and my metabolism makes it look like I haven't eaten in a while, that your girlfriend told me she'd rather take bong rips of pesticide than discuss the plight of the Northern Spotted Owl, whatever. But to spend forty-five seconds pretending to be interested in the contents of what I'm pushing isn't doing either of us any good.

Street canvassers, the good ones, don't have the vaguest interest in the causes we promote. The real idealists – energized, new-adult faces with genuinely pleading eyes – never last. They'd rather spend their formative years scraping organic matter off the walls of a drained dolphin rehabilitation tank than hustling yuppies and guilty college kids who have discovered social consciousness as a side effect of a two-day coke hangover. And that's cool. Because it is a hustle. Community Crusades, Inc. is a for-profit company, meaning that nonprofits pay us millions of dollars a year to run fundraising drives on their behalf, funds that tend to vanish after expenses. I'm required to begin my spiel by explaining to you that I'm a "paid fundraiser for grassroots campaigns," but all that stuff Robbie tells us to spew about "one hundred percent" going to the nonprofit is exactly what it sounds like: dolphin shit.

The position didn't require a resume. I wouldn't have known what to put on one anyways. Two-and-a-half degree-less years at a state school with a moderately storied basketball program? As far as extracurriculars go, getting date-raped and ODing isn't particularly noteworthy or uncommon, although I guess it doesn't usually happen in that order.

Under the Required Skills & Experience section in Community Crusades' Craigslist ad all it said was that they were looking for local candidates "who enjoy interacting with people, are stable, have a great attitude, and care about our planet!" Bonus points for customer service experience, the ability to "overcome objections," and weekend availability. The correct combination of Xanax and Starbucks solves all the world's problems and my interview with Robbie went stellar, mostly due to my embarrassing knowledge of contemporary major-network sitcoms – thanks Netflix courtesy of Karen, my dental hygienist big sis, she of the disposable income! We spent way more time discussing the inherent pathological slant in each of the major character dynamics in Modern Family than whether I could convince some ADHD-stricken fool on the street about the imminent perils of ozone depletion.

But yeah, pity talkers. No bueno. The only one I ever really let get the better of me was the Park Ranger. He has a name, a fake one he told me once, but I never think of him as anything less than the total sum of what he was, or what he believed himself to be.

The first words he said to me, over a year ago when I was out canvassing for a group that plants saplings in deforested wetlands: "I love making broken things beautiful."

From a potential donor standpoint, that's a cue to start scanning the street for the nearest law enforcement personnel. As a pick-up line it was creepy but unique. We went to a falafel spot and had coffee and he started talking, a bunch of random life trivia. Growing up in North Carolina in a woodsy pit-stop town near a major hiking thoroughfare. Encountering a massive whitetail deer in a rut the first time he got stoned off his ass and how he knew he'd found his "animal spirit guide." His current job cleaning up after hikers and repairing trail shelters in the mountains of New Hampshire. He kept tugging at this gingerbread beard that reminded me of a kind of out-of-control lichen that would grow on the trees at the lake upstate where my family used to camp sometimes. Meaning, sort of cute. I didn't ask what he was doing in the city or why he was still wearing his beige and olive National Park Service uniform.

"There are small moments," he said out of nowhere. "And sometimes I think that's all there is."

I was like, "Cool, so are you having any good ones now?"

He sipped the latte he'd bought and made these weird grimace-smiles that looked like he either had a low tolerance for coffee or was wrapping his mind around something that had been a long time coming, jumper-cabled in irregular bursts and starts. He told me he had to catch a bus, that he had to get back to work. I got his number (he didn't ask for mine) and was sidling up for an awkward goodbye hug and he just shrugged back, took out a small, wilted brochure from his pocket, pressed it into my hand. The cover had an illustration of a guy who looked kind of like him but with a backpack and walking stick, wearing shorts and standing in the foreground above a valley with waterfalls, pixelated sunset, generic nature clipart.

"I like your smile lines," he said. "They remind me of a stream bed that's never tasted acid rain. Great biodiversity."

He left the restaurant.

I stood there for a while, uhhhh.

I looked at the brochure. Thinking about how many like it I'd stuffed into commute-sweated palms, how many I'd seen tossed seconds later into sidewalk receptacles, how few I'd actually read beyond the cover.

I bought another coffee, sat down.

It was a beginner's guide to the Appalachian Trail. Figured. But the more I forced myself to skim, the more I found myself getting into it, even though the pages were mostly just maps. I traced the 2,200 miles from Springer Mountain in Georgia to Mount Katahdin in Maine, passing through fourteen states in mostly wilderness with the occasional trail town, road, or river. The text boxes about section-hikers, thru-hikers, purists who follow the white blazes (the tree markings that denote the official trail), blue blazers who take mostly negligible shortcuts, and the yellow blazers, gentrified pussies who try to hitchhike whenever things get a little rough.

I'd always been more into oceans and marine life, the vast unknown spaces and all that jazz, even did some nonprofit work in a former life I'd rather forget. But the more I read, the more I kept getting these visuals, kind of like tripping, but really clear snapshots – a patchwork of light-slivers through pine boughs illuminating a root-gnarled trail twisting around a bend to nowhere, mud-wrenched legs hugging a precipice overhanging a cobalt snake-skin river, a flame-bright meadow of flowers refracted and expanding in a dewdrop's mirror. The feeling of being welcomed by a vastness, a bird-flung other-world drowned in the pleasant ache of a sleeping bag, spiking and fading within a clock-less biorhythm of slumber and movement, the absence of anything besides my thoughts, my lungs, the land.

Meaning, not having to approach assholes and near-dementia retirees on the street.

At home I burned through Wikipedia pages, websites of various conservancy groups, digital backpacker magazines, mostly useless personal blogs. I figured out how much it would cost to do the entire trail in one season, what kind of sleeping and cooking gear I'd need, preparatory cardio regimens, proper poop disposal. I bought maps and marked the trail towns where I'd need to re-up on food and take a shower. Where to buy high-energy snacks, water filters, flashlight batteries, first-aid stuff, a whistle (three blasts is the international signal for help). Most of the cold-weather stuff I'd take from the room that used to be my sister's.

I made a list of everything that could go wrong, researched fatality statistics, looked at pictures of compound fractures and gangrene fingernails and rotting abscesses caused by spider bites. Heat stroke, lightning strikes, diarrhea, foot blisters, biting flies, and tick-borne diseases, all the negligible hazards. Pretending to be a gung-ho martyr is a lot like getting mauled by a bear, only much more wasteful. At least as a meat product, one hundred percent of my energy would go directly toward sustaining life.

It was good to have a goal, an end-point, one that might kill me before I reached it.

That made me feel better.

I called the Park Ranger a couple weeks later during a lunch break. What was I was going to tell him? That him giving me the brochure had catalyzed what was starting to become a potentially unfeasible obsession? That I'd developed hiking fever and could he help me feed the flame? That I wanted to apply for the National Park Service and call dibs on a personal lean-to where I could cook Ramen noodles and canned hash every night and listen to the delicate, non-human majesty of bullfrog mating rituals?

"I'm back in town," he said, after I reminded him who I was (she of the exceptional biodiversity). He happened to be staying at a friend's apartment a few blocks from where I was canvassing. I asked him if he wanted to do something later and if it would be cool if I could just come over to his friend's place after work and drop my shit off so I wouldn't have to go back to my car.

The building was a gray-brick, six-story walk-up, a little gross. Non-existent buzzer, walked right in, blunt-gut and Cheetos-dust stairwell, aromas of curry and something that struck me as vaguely Caribbean, though I couldn't say why. The fourth floor rumbled with the bass-fracking and booze-hoots of someone's day off, adjacent to the apartment where the Park Ranger told me he'd be. He opened the door, scowled.

You know how when you walk into a place or a situation where something is off, where it feels like you've stepped into an oblong distortion of the reality you expected, that cartoon thing should happen where the needle scratches off the record and everything freezes and goes silent? Meaning, at the very least your fight-or-flight should kick in to the point where you realize you need to make a decision and act on it?

Maybe I'd been so inundated with googled hiking propaganda and my visions of what form my personal journey would take that the studio, lit only by a popular LED lantern model I'd been thinking about purchasing, didn't faze me as much as it probably should have.

There was no TV, sofa, table. Any refrigerator or microwave had been ripped from the windowless back wall long ago. Most of the ceiling was covered in garlands of dried wildflowers. I recognized bluets, jewel weed, columbine, and lady's-slipper. Fallen petals carpeted the hardwood floor. Huge trail map print-outs covered multiple walls, different colored tacks marking who knows what. Posters and photos of whitetail does and fawns, beaver dams, swimming moose, hourglass-banded copperheads, undulating ridges capped with snow, tunnels of greenery and autumn-scarred scenic overlooks – orgasms of nature.

The Park Ranger – same uniform, beard still a nest – motioned me to where someone had set up an MSR Hubba two-person tent (highly recommended by veteran trail enthusiasts) and adjacent to it, a portable cooking stove and pot system surrounded by a semi-circle of what looked like lacquered tree stumps.

"Take a seat," he said. He disappeared into the tent and reemerged holding a pair of mugs.

I was trying to figure out how to fit the majority of my ass on a chunk of wood that appeared to be stolen from a kindergarten classroom. The mug he handed me was blue with writing that said Keep Calm and Think of Mountains. A brownish green teabag inside. The Park Ranger flicked a lighter and the stove ignited, flames stroking the underside of the lidded metal pot.

I noticed a large, flowerless gap on the ceiling, directly above the ring of stumps. Black burn marks in a circular pattern.

"Is this set-up covered by your friend's renter's insurance? His super must love you."

"Chamomile," he said, squinting at his mug.

I still couldn't tell if he was truly autistic or if this was his preferred style of fucking around with near-strangers. Either way, the appeal had almost evaporated. But I had trail-related questions, stuff I couldn't find online, and he was the closest thing to an expert I had.

"So I want to do a thru-hike next summer," I said, "the entire trail, one season."

His brain fog lifted, injection-quick, an excited beard tug. "You liked the brochure? I thought you might connect with it. Did you have any questions?"

I started spitting them out while I had his attention, tried to ignore the smell of spoiled fruit wafting from the tent and the absence of an obvious bathroom. I asked him how expensive the trip would actually be (way more than the budget I'd allotted, of course), the towns and states with the cheapest resupply stores (Tennessee's Smoky Mountains and the Grayson Highlands in Virginia were apparently populated by generous souls while Connecticut was understandably "rife with yuppie indifference"), the ideal ratio of carbs-to-protein based on my body-mass index. When it came to less concrete, opinion-related fodder, like what was his favorite type of rock formation to dry off on after a particularly sweaty stretch or to warm up on during a sunrise, he was nebulous but weirdly inspirational: "It's true that you become what you absorb, but you have to remember that your heart is stronger than anything you take from the sky."

As we were talking the pot started making bubble sounds. The Park Ranger poured steaming water into my mug, then his. My nostrils gorged on a sweet, crisp brightness, wild herbs hidden beneath a moonlit treescape.

He sipped. "So, who's your partner?"

"I'm single."

He snickered. "OK, but who is going to be hiking with you?"

No one. That was the point. I hadn't really considered that most people wouldn't want to be totally alone in the woods for more than half a year. That pit stops at communal shelters and trail towns were more like sanity-sustaining re-immersions into the hobbit-stink matrix of mountain society than ordeals to be relished with the fondness of a root canal. Even the Park Ranger had at least one likeminded friend, whoever's place this was.

"No one."

I sipped. The tea was strong. Those two words in my throat sweetened it.

"Well if it's your first time and you're going solo," the Park Ranger said, "you're going to need some trail magic."

"Trail magic."

"It can be anything really," he said, "big or small, sometimes a beer, a bottle of water, maybe your blisters are acting up and there's a tube of bacitracin someone's left for you at an abandoned fire site. An act of kindness from one hiker to another when you didn't know you needed one. Happens all the time. Maybe you sprain your ankle and, out of nowhere, someone out on a day trip shows up with a set of car keys and GPS to find the nearest clinic. That's a trail angel. You'll want to meet a few of those."

He finished the tea in a gulp, the runoff forming tributaries down his face, his eyes lidded, heavier.

I took another sip. Other faces and random plastic gifts had been pleasantly absent from my trail visualizations. The idea that reliance on handouts wouldn't stop once I quit Community Crusades started working its way down my esophagus, corroding. "So you're saying there are all these littering Samaritans lurking everywhere, who get off on just abandoning supplies that they might actually need themselves? I call B.S. When you want to pretend to care you give money, it's quick and a tax write-off. There has to be some other motivation. How many angels are really just looking for a thank-you blowie in a pastoral setting?"

I followed the Park Ranger's gaze to the back of the apartment, to a red and white gingham shirt I hadn't noticed nailed to the wall, its sleeves crucified, outstretched. A smudge of undecipherable rust-colored crud obscuring the left breast pocket. Above, where a person's head would be if they were wearing the shirt, hung a pair of deer antlers wreathed in either dried grass or really blonde hair.

I took a sip of tea, crossed my legs.

"I found her when I first started clearing trails and working on shelters in New Hampshire," he said. "A couple college students had called into the station, reported her creeping around where they'd made a campsite. My supervisor told me to check it out, probably a harmless tweaker lost in the woods, wanted me to make sure she didn't have any kids or anything, if we needed to send up some EMTs. I hiked to where she was supposed to be, an area that had been mostly cleared and mulched, and sure enough she was there, wrapped in a filthy white sundress, hugging herself under a large dogwood. It was late September and freezing rain was in the forecast. I called out and she spooked, rabbit-fast, took off into the trees. It was surprising to see something so small and skinny run like that. I left my jacket and a couple oranges.

"I came back the next day and she was sitting in the same spot, wearing the jacket and tossing an orange between her palms. I approached and she took off again, but this time I could see her watching me behind some undergrowth. Wild and shining hair, eyes large and clear blue. This went on for weeks. I'd bring shirts, sweaters, boots, a tarp, kindling when it got colder, jerky, water bottles, granola. The food she wouldn't touch – there was a growing pile of wrappers and plastic under the tree – but she'd take everything else. Where, I don't know. It got to the point where I'd almost be able to hand her the packages before she sprinted off, could smell her, could touch her breath.

"One day she didn't run. She was waiting, holding the antlers. 'Never lose it,' she said when she placed them on the ground in front of me and backed away into the trees. How could she know how important the deer, the idea of what the antlers meant, was to me? But walking back to the station I began to understand the truth she had taught me. When you give pieces of yourself to the forest, you become the forest. You become part of something bigger, something that feeds you, heals you. You never lose it. I only saw her once more after that."

I looked into the mug, the teabag pulsating in the gunk that remained. A slight thud in my chest, a thickness

"That's, uh, nice."

Then a buzzing that was both auditory and physical, like being bathed in a high-pitched white noise strong enough to make the hair on my arms pucker.

Unexpected but not unfamiliar.

"It's why I chose you," he was staring at me but his eyes were kind of rolling around, spindly. "Because I knew you needed it. The trail. But also because I knew your spirit was a pristine ecosystem. You'd want to become a part of the forest."

"Chose me?"

I tried to steady myself, tried to swing my neck around a little, tried to focus on something I'd just noticed in one corner of the room: a pile of beige and olive pants and shirts, thrift-store-beaten, an open shoebox containing what looked like various park service patches and different nametags, sewing needles, several spools of black thread.

"I have something for your trip," the Park Ranger was saying as he stagger-crawled into the tent, clumsy and failing to zip up the door flap all the way. "Don't look yet."

Above the increasingly loud buzzing, metal on metal, a vague pressurized release.

*

It doesn't matter that, as far as I know, the Park Ranger didn't try to touch me or take off my clothes or follow me down the stairwell when I stood up, stumbled to the unbolted apartment door and pushed through it without saying anything. That it took me two hours to find my car and another hour of pulling the trigger and heaving in a McDonald's bathroom until I felt clearheaded enough to drive. That the name he'd given me wasn't in any National Park Service employee database or that the apartment wasn't registered with the city's housing division. That I didn't eat for three days and came tantalizingly close to getting fired. That I couldn't stop thinking about the red shirt with the smudge, the antlers.

None of it matters.

Because it's been over a year since that latest debacle and it's past happy hour and I'm still standing near the awkward center of the sidewalk clutching the binder, my hair sagging with moisture against the collar of my florescent shirt.

Because nobody, including me, gives a shit about Croatian orphans or whoever I'm supposed to be championing.

Because I still haven't saved close to enough money for a proper thru-hike and my car is about to die.

Because Robbie's idea of being a competent regional coordinator includes sending dozens of text messages every day like the one I just got: "'Success is the ability to go from failure to failure without losing your enthusiasm' – Winston Churchill."

Meaning, fuck.

More rain droplets roll from my forehead into the corners of both eyes. I'm unable to prevent them from entering, from dancing across my corneas in defiance, turning the flickering shapes on the street into a mass of tiny horned creatures that want nothing more than to bury their jaws into my skin. I crash into one as I try to fight my way to the edge of the sidewalk and she curses and I'm rubbing, shaking, slapping, and continuing to do so until the shock of contact has been removed.

But the damage has been done. Squinting the liquid off my face, I feel the venom surging through my body, the years of tiny bites, so close together, so sunk in with time that I imagine red lines have been etched beneath my arteries. My marrow starts to burn with these parallel and perpendicular lines, with lines intersecting to create a prism that's only red, closed, no chance for any other colors to enter.

I need a beer, a bottle of water, a tube of bacitracin.

Anything to stop the burning.

A tall shape extracts itself from the howling din, pauses, steps toward me. Smiling, calm, his yellow hair illuminated in a street light's halo. Blue and white checkered shirt.

"Hey, ah, Marissa?" He's skinnier than I remember, older, healthy 401(k) gleam, no more fake-diamond ear studs.

The same too-thick wrists.

And the name's wrong, though he's close.

"Marissa in Kappa, right? You lived with Kelsey Donovan freshman year? Didn't –"

I tuck my binder between my arm and hip, turn and start moving toward the park, the belching plastic chimney, the bums. Remembering the brochure the Park Ranger gave me, I try to follow the main path, the white blazes. But it's totally dark now and the mist keeps getting thicker.

And it keeps raining bodies, so many bodies between here and where I need to be.

How to Find a Flock

He would come home from bartending to his basement apartment and sit in his office chair and look out the porthole at the courtyard that was really three brick walls facing each other, a grimed-out, pointless nook carved into the backside of the building. It only got natural light in the mornings, according to Liz, and (also according to Liz) was spackled with the kind of standard city refuse that, under the right conditions, might be responsible for the deaths of certain shore birds and most species of lesser shelled reptiles. He would wake up around two in the afternoon, when shadows accumulated faster than trash bags chucked from the roofs of adjacent buildings, and, making sure Liz wasn't there, twist his slightly webbed feet back and forth and look at them.

He would say things to himself and laugh and sometimes tweet them and hope others would laugh. Sometimes one of the handful or so friends with whom he kept in semi-regular contact would email or text him, asking about the tweets, asking how he was doing, if everything was okay, and he would respond, asking the friend if he or she wanted to meet for a beer or a coffee. Sometimes they would meet for a few beers or whiskeys (never coffee) but usually they wouldn't.

He would bare his teeth, faux-dramatic behind the window, at mongoloid pigeons bathing in Whole Foods wreckage and Tupperware streaked with non-hydrogenated soybean oil, at the pair of rats and an earless cat sipping from the same Dr. Pepper puddle in a grudging silence that befitted their larger African cousins, at the condom wrappers – which always seemed to be Magnums – those golden totems of fertility strewn across the murk-lit concrete. He would walk to the hardware store and buy half a dozen canisters of rat spray, maybe a commercial-grade dustpan or a vacuuming apparatus. He would turn on the TV and watch people, who for the most part had non-weird extremities, and forget about the cleaning. He would go into the kitchen and look in the pantry for sunflower seeds, not remembering he had left the porthole in his room open and that it was still open.

Liz came over sometimes, usually from 11pm to 7am on the two or three nights a week he didn't bartend. Or she'd cab it to the bar when she finished up at the museum where she was a conservator, restoring nineteenth-century lithographs by scalding them, gently, in alkaline solutions of varying pronounceability. She never wanted them to go back to her place because she liked to "bring my work home," a phrase she would utter with such an uncharacteristically foreboding lilt that he didn't dare to question what it meant. Her recent projects had been Audubon's, The Fowls of California or something like that. He'd been introduced to her at a bar (not the one where he worked) by a mutual friend, a software engineer named Kaitlyn who was chief amongst the concerned emailers, without first seeing a profile picture of Liz or even an unfocused group shot, which made the after-hours grope-fest that first night and the subsequent ones seem pleasantly retro.

Liz would be sitting at a booth, drinking whatever he served her, swiping emails on her phone, occasionally glancing at a catalogue of art featuring romanticized wildlife, and after last call and after the barback went home he'd lock up and they'd engage in

41

rushed, friction-y pre-fuck acts in the employees restroom. They'd cab it to his apartment.

He liked that her hair, under the saccharine glow of the reading lamp he'd duct-taped to the bed frame, burned like November leaves. He liked the panic dancing behind her Klonopin eyes when she talked about the Chinese retail boom "stupendously fucking up, like, all of our ecological footprints," about the biohazard suit hanging in her closet just in case. Her sinewy scrubbed-naked nails digging under his clavicle, the non-webbed toes wriggling against his thighs.

Her ultra-pale whiskey cheeks flushed in pixel-light.

"Your skin is like, lunatic-beautiful," he said to her one night, impersonating a character in a show where, according to her IMDb app, menopausal matriarchs balanced "envious social calendars, challenging careers, and motherhood, with the hustle and bustle of the big city all around."

But also he meant it. He was staring at the courtyard.

She laughed without looking up from her phone. "If you're ever going to start cleaning up back there," she said, "make sure you get the milk jugs and those gross seed bags somebody covered in shrink-wrap." She sighed. "They're primarily composed of polyethylene, which, oh god, has a half-life of like fifty years. And you left the TV on again."

He looked at his feet. He looked at Liz. He told himself that her skin was beautiful.

One day he decided to call in sick and surprise her at the museum. He wasn't sure what time her job normally ended so he sat near the bottom of the massive, Greek temple-ish front steps and looked at two vaguely Scandinavian guys fighting over a subway map folded over to reveal a blurry ad with the words JOIN THE RAINBOW PILGRIMAGE in a bold sans-serif. He bought a falafel from one of the nearby food carts. He ate it and balled the aluminum foil wrapper and was going to chuck it at an obese squirrel whose diet probably consisted solely of halal food and hot dogs, when he remembered Liz reading him a study proving that aluminum was crappy at disintegrating in non-landfill settings and caused Alzheimer's in fur-bearing lab creatures. He looked around for a trash can before giving up and dropping the ball between his feet.

A humpbacked woman whose body type closely resembled the squirrel's and a scrawny kid were camped out on a bench near the bottom of the stairs, interacting with a swarm of sparrows, pigeons, a trio of slack-winged gulls. The woman – ethnically ambiguous, dreadlocked, surrounded by a fortress of Baby Gap bags whose handles had seen several rounds of duct-tape reinforcement – cradled a Costco-size container of generic cheddar popcorn and was tossing kernels at snapping beaks, occasionally shoving a small fistful into her own mouth and wiping her hands on a greasy earth-toned v-neck. The equally grubbed kid (her grand/son?) would snatch uneaten popcorn from the pavement, hold out his dirt-browned palm. One unlucky sparrow with a broken leg or some sort of avian degenerative condition limped too close and the kid snatched it up, squealed happily, and started petting it as it tried to peck itself free. The woman just sat there, perma-smiling, wiping yellow-orange residue on her shirt and the exposed part of her globular chest.

He was still kind of staring when Liz exited the museum, accompanied by a young-looking poster boy for gentrification in ball-squelching slacks and neon-rimmed sunglasses – a coworker? Friend? He'd met no one in either camp. Liz saw him wave and froze, unconsciously reached for the place in her purse where she kept her phone.

They embraced, an awkward cheek-kiss-hug thing. Her neck smelled of hydrogen peroxide. She calmed down when he apologized for the "pseudo-stalker routine" and she smiled and introduced him to Michael, an assistant director of institutional development with inverted shoulders and a chemo-smooth complexion. They shook hands, noodle-soft, and Michael shuddered when he noticed the bench and its cheese-dust menagerie.

Liz gestured toward the street and the crush of traffic, suggesting the three of them share a cab. As they walked, he kept turning to look at the bench woman who was now giggling loudly, tossing popcorn in a high arc toward where the kid was crouching on all fours, growling and competing with the biggest gull to see who could mouth snatch more kernels out of the air; the kid was winning. The sparrow with the bum leg, lying on the ground a few feet away, had stopped twitching.

"I, uh, forgot a file," Michael mumbled, wiping his shaken hand across his thigh. "I have to get it. You guys have...fun." He sprinted back up the steps.

"Did you drop something?" Liz asked as they got into a cab. "You're swiveling like the owl in the print I was working on today. Do you have a crush on Michael? He'd probably be into it."

"Nada, baby," he said, impersonating someone but he couldn't remember who.

She mumbled something he couldn't hear, snickered, and stared at her phone for most of the ride uptown. Later they drank whiskeys while watching TV, got each other off, and went to sleep.

When he woke up, it was still early, the sunlight streaming in two parallel beams from cracks in the porthole shade. One of them snaked across Liz's mostly uncovered body: hair that looked dull and gnarled, too-sloped breasts, asymmetrical fingers clutching shards of blanket. An ashen, hollow quality to the skin he'd never noticed, like days-old linen that had been hand-smoothed and folded to hide the inevitable purchase of stains.

The lingering synthetic waft.

Outside, there was a loud shrill, a noise that reminded him of something he'd heard the previous day outside of the museum. But he wasn't sure if it was the same species or a bird at all. Then he heard a response. He crept to the porthole, slipped his hand under the shade and palmed the warm glass. He stood over the bed.

"I'm going outside," he whispered. Liz mumbled something that sounded like Asperger-sandwich and rolled over. "I'm going to sit in the courtyard." He twisted her ankle, gently. "When I get back, you need to not be here, okay?"

Better Than Ever

Carly gripped the wet, limpid bases, tugged with her other hand up the shafts and shucked the heads in a brutal twist of fingers. She gripped and shucked, gripped and shucked until what had once been a cluster of carnations grouped together to form a single flower-like structure was now a petal-stained mess saturating the coffee table. Gripping the largest stem at its severed top, she squeezed out a dollop of whatever passed for plant blood and placed the discharge on her tongue.

She watched the whole process in the fogged mirror of a dead flatscreen that was perched across the room next to the loveseat where he'd forgotten a sock with a nautical pattern and a MetroCard during his predawn stumble-out.

She watched the sap dispel. The opening of lips, the disappearing.

Partially buried under the wilting clumps, her phone began to blink and vibrate, the so-sorry texts arriving sooner than expected. Today had been something different though, impossible to reconcile with bursts of well-polished, 160-character apologia. He had to realize that.

Johnny's surface was a series of credibly two-dimensional plotlines and moderately appealing asides that circled at a constant drone, cannibalizing any kind of meaningful underbelly she might try to extract. The generically athletic shoulders and no-filter jaw that had secured him part-time bouncer work at a cocktail lounge where thin-wristed foodie bloggers paid seventeen dollars to be told which kind of artisanal ice cube complemented their palettes and where no one ever got bounced. The other gig as a work-from-home copy editor for a lifestyle website focusing on motherhood where he corrected typos in articles about the struggles of getting children to brush their teeth regularly and wrote headlines like Do You Ever Wish Life Would Give You a Second Chance to Achieve Your Dreams? The claims that it was all fodder for the novel he'd been working on since grad school that was currently languishing on the flash drive attached to his keychain and that he wouldn't talk about.

Everything he told her seemed smoothed over, externalized. She seldom got more than the smallest glimpse of who he really was, underneath it all.

And that was okay, at first. Because that was what you did. You would study communications, merchandizing, and the Tumblr of every notable shoe enthusiast at a middle-tier liberal arts college in a state with shittier than normal winters so you could land – through the help of your cousin's power-bottom boyfriend – a lower-rung position in fashion PR and move to the city with the majority of your "independent" and "edgy" friends. You would co-sign the lease on a studio in the farthest reaches of the Upper East Side (don't call it Harlem) where your father would contribute half the rent, and even though somewhere downtown would have been better, at least it was Manhattan and not Astoria or Bushwick because fuck if your parents were going to let you skank it up around the outer boroughs. You wouldn't mind your status as a sixty-hour-a-week coffee-errand peon because you would get to wear cute outfits and grab craploads of gift bags at client events and always have random shit to complain about at happy hour. Complaining would make you feel like things-were-happening. If you had to, you could fend off the inevitable mid-twenties emptiness by getting a masters degree in an existentially fulfilling field like social work or urban planning. But you would never let it come to that. You and your expanding network of amigas would scour your expanding collection of apps and find places to eat, booze, and watch people doing things that were rated highly by reviewers in your particular demographic. You would cross-reference these findings on group emails and make your social decisions based on them. You would go out more often than not. You would listen to electronic dance music, at first out of curiosity. You would read in a YouTube description that the music appealed to people because "Trance, Dub Step, and drum bass all have the ability to provoke deep thought and induce deep-feeling emotion." You would love the beats more after a bowl pack or a couple lines. You would attend as many electronic dance music performances as possible because they gave you the opportunity to wear minimalist attire loosely inspired by previous bohemian sects – cutoff denim shorts, neon-tinted aviators, maybe a florescent floral headband – as long as it was "neutral,"

51

"eclectic," and/or "earthy." The concerts would seem like a more inclusive, Disneyfied version of the raves you'd been warned about when AIDS was still a viable scare tactic for grade-schoolers. You would go to a show at a pop-up venue and see him dancing by the speaker tower, alone, shirtless and wearing a neon snap-back and Wayfarers and you would look at him and not think he saw you but when you turned you would feel him move behind you in time with the beat, smell his Dentyne mouth asking if you knew his friend Molly and you would shrug and pretend to be oblivious and you would be dancing, dancing for a long time and not remembering the ride up the West Side Highway except for the reggaeton song he would yell at the driver to change, reeling hours later from the vodka (and yes, the Molly), nestling against his perma-shirtless chest and smiling in time with his snore-bursts. You wouldn't be concerned if he didn't text for a few days because he said he was a writer (which was sort of kind of like an artist) and was loath to leave the inspiration provided by his single-futon, probably mildewed apartment. You would accept the mildew because he was the kind of worthwhile, fascinatingly obscure project you had moved to the city for, mumbling about prehistoric extraterrestrial moon bases and the Singularity at night and waking you up to jarring-in-a-good-way, foul-breathed, half-awake, finger-induced orgasms and later some deeper ones, then turning over and muttering that no he wouldn't want to get food before you got on the subway and that yes he needed to go back to sleep before work. You would accept this arrangement until he stopped accepting it, until he would make the decision to be more than the guy from Washington Heights you were "kind of seeing" when you left your friends at the bar sniggering into their guavatinis and finally opened himself, whatever that might mean. You would hope it involved a light emotional breakdown that you could wink-wink to your friends about. And maybe you would go together to the new place on East Houston that served smoked free-range elk tacos after checking out a not-too-touristy museum/cultural landmark/park. And maybe you would go to enough places together and do enough things that your experiences would start to feel like one big ball of shared-ness. And maybe he would stop untagging your Facebook photos. And maybe after a while he would move into your non-mildewed studio and your parents would be cool with it because he would pull a major one-eighty from the scruff life and start thinking about law school and you would be going back to school too but more importantly it would be at the same school and your class schedules would be coordinated, and maybe you would feel like you were finally making something bigger than what you had.

It was what you did.

But there would never be any hangover bagels, she realized a few months in, no brunches, no hot air balloon rides upstate ("Scared of heights and wicker," he'd deadpanned during a particularly gruesome afternoon-after when all the inside Gchat jokes she'd cultivated had started to fall flat). They would only exist together in the non-ironic dive bars he always seemed to veer towards when they broke off from their respective after-hours posses. Or in the parched darkness of beds whose pleasure had been replaced more often than not by a discomfort that came out of nowhere and seeped everywhere.

But that was okay, too. There was coffee scheduled with the parole officer and former fireman who was also heir to her parents' favorite Cuban restaurant back in Poughkeepsie, and who had been described by her mother as "your classic door-holder and seat-helper, Pierce Brosnan meets Joe the Plumber." There were more impending dates with Ryan, an analyst at Bank of America whom she'd met on Happn or J-Date or somewhere and who, even though he was tighter than the shirt buttons he never seemed to want to unfasten (not that she wanted him to unfasten them just yet), was kind of endearing in a way that satisfied what she imagined as her settled, future-tense self. And Ryan always magically seemed to take her to places that coincided with her foodie and booze bucket lists. The ebbs and flows of "possibilities" were why she moved to the city. Duh. It-was-what-you-did.

As expected, the late-night hookup voicemails and later, slurrier texts trickled to nothing a week or three after she stopped responding. She blocked his status updates from her news feed. She stopped reading electronic dance music blogs. He would recede into the post-college murk, a soggy-yet-necessary learning tool.

Then, last night. The phone in a constant state of seizure on the coffee table as she changed into sweatpants and a wifebeater and waited for the Bagel Bites to heat up. She assumed it was Ryan, trying to apologize for the awkwardness an hour earlier at a new fois gras and grilled cheese bistro in Hell's Kitchen. She'd refused, for maybe the sixth time in as many dinners, Ryan's suggestion that they take a car to his condo in Jersey to check out his makeshift closet/cellar filled with "like three out of the top five most full-bodied Argentinean reds," but instead of the usual sad-puppy grimace and fumble for a conciliatory make-out before parting, she had been backhanded by the harder slap of disinterested silence.

After wiping the perspiration from his peach-fuzz scalp, Ryan had carefully peeled the requisite cash from his money clip and dropped it on the open check folder with mechanized poise. He'd waited a beat for a response that never came, then rose and headed for the exit, recalibrating, prowl-ready for a new investment.

The phone kept vibrating and blinking. She picked it up, braced.

Seven texts, twice as many missed calls, four voicemails. Before she could start sorting through the data blast, he called again. She let the Daft Punk ringtone play a while, instinctively looking for an excuse not to pick up: the cheese-sopped aroma of the almost-done Bagel Bites; that Johnny had probably been "team-building" with his fellow bar employees until the Cuervo tequila his stereotypically coked-out manager allotted them had run dry; the need to be at least caffeine-coherent in the morning.

But streaming over everything in monolithic all-caps like the stock quotes that must have flowed on every elevator TV in the Bank of America Tower were two words: FUCK IT. And she had sort of pulled a protracted Ryan-esque move on him, albeit not as douchey. She might as well see what he wanted.

"What's up. Did you just get off your –"

"HEY! Uhhh, I miss you..." Breaths and dead space. The lilt of tequila, of more than a few key bumps.

"You sound –"

"LISTEN! Are you home I need to come up, need to give you..."

"Where are you?"

Giggles. "Listen, I hope you're not going to take this the...I'm outside your building, across the street," then, faux-ominous, "looking in."

"What are you going to give me?"

"A, uh, so you are home? I promise it will be quick. I just want to see you and give you, uhh –"

"Do you know where to find the buzzer or do you need directions?"

Huffing from the five-story walk-up, Johnny shimmied around the door she'd left cracked. His bouncer gear – a rumpled sports jacket and slacks that didn't really match in a way that she always thought of as cutely post-fraternal. He shoved an overstuffed, moisture-starved bouquet of red, white, and yellow flowers into her chest and shuffled into the kitchen without speaking. He'd bought them at one of the cat-piss delis around the corner, the $9.99 sticker half torn from the plastic covering. He emerged from the kitchen, cockeyed and grinning with Bagel Bite residue on his chin, clutching the giant pink commemorative cup that had One Last Ride for THE BRIDE embellished with stupid green and blue curly-cues, a bachelorette party souvenir now sloshing with tap water.

"They'll fit in here," he said, impressed with his ingenuity.

Her smile crinkled, and his eyes – though booze-wobbled, bloodshot – returned it, matching his lippy smirk. Which for the first time didn't feel like a smirk but something warmer, reciprocal, need and want intertwining in a way that would have seemed facetious a month ago. And still kind of did – he was shitfaced.

She wouldn't let herself get carried away but she would lead him to the bed, plop him and the flowers down simultaneously, and hand him a bottle of Café Patron that she'd taken from the opening of a high-end, Mexican-owned eyebrow threading spa her company had curated. She would go to the bathroom and when she came back he would still be struggling to take his shoes off but would perk up when she sat next to him. Instead of another no-interruption rant about the validity of a gray-matter apocalypse brought on by faulty nanomachines, he would ask her how she'd been doing or something equally innocuous (but pleasant) and she wouldn't remember her response but she would notice how his eyes followed her in between tidy and infrequent slugs from the bottle and how he seemed content to just sit there next to her and she wouldn't stiffen up when he scooted closer or when he placed the bottle into her lap and she could taste pizza sauce when she took a sip and he would sit there listening and this would seem like something that might make sense again and he would lift the bottle out of her hand but hesitate and smile again and she would fall back and pull him in and he would start at her neck and work his way down and she would stare at the stucco pre-war ceiling tiles that had always struck her as tacky and stagnant but which would now pulsate, pupil-quick.

And he would pass out while struggling to take her sweatpants off, mid-tug, faceplanting softly into her pelvis.

After several immobile minutes she reached over to check her phone. The oldest text was a reminder about a deadline for a press release she hadn't begun to think about. The rest, him. The first two were stellar examples of the jitter-whacked mobile word-rendering – "Leathery O'the fracking apartment!!#=" – she had come to know well. She grinned, mussed his dirty blond hair and he grunted in agreeable semi-consciousness.

Then, the third text: YOU ARE BEING A CUNT.

That he'd been able to figure out the caps lock and managed to spell each word right – not to mention the syntax and the period – when his previous attempts were a garble of autocorrect backwash, seemed impossible. It had to be a kind of fucked up butt-dial situation, a dickism meant for one of his friends.

The remaining half-dozen or so texts were no less precise, the letters separated by bruising, intentional dashes:

C-U-N-T

C-U-N-T

C-U-N-T

C-U-N-T

C-U-N-T

C-U-N-T

C-U-N-T

The open-palmed half-thwack to his temple seemed weak in comparison to most of the cinematic examples she'd tried to emulate, but when his neck went slack she almost felt sorry for doing it. Until he sort of woke up and resumed trying to shimmy her pants off. The knee to his solar plexus was sharper, air-knocking. He crumbled backward, cartoon-splayed, wheeling around the room, incapable of balance, finding the loveseat and sprawling across it, gagging. She cocooned herself under a blanket and pillow until she heard his breathing slow, the ruffle of shoes and a staggering to the door, probably leaving handprints where he'd used the air-conditioner-misted window for support.

She emailed her manager to tell her she wouldn't be coming in and tried to sleep and kept half-imagining someone who looked like Ryan seated across from her in a vague approximation of the indigenous Peruvian gastro pub they'd been to last week, picking at a roasted Guinea pig thigh, wearing a neon tank-top under his suit jacket, scalp covered in thorns, mouth silently mouthing You're being a, you're being a, his nutcracker jaw disengaging with the rest of his face and bursting into thousands of plastic seed pods blinking in the well-lit, manufactured ambiance.

*

She took the stem out of her mouth and checked her phone. Work emails, none urgent. A text from Brenda, her desk-mate: "If you're feeling better later, let's do lunch :)" accompanied by a link to a Thrillist article about Krispy Kreme Sloppy Joes. The drone of the air conditioner muddled the post-morning-rush quiet. She noticed a river of yoga tights and work blouses overflowing the closet door. She inhaled something percolating in the kitchen nook that wasn't quite gag-worthy yet, but still gross.

She would start with the carnations. Sweep the already-wilting petals into a manageable pile with her hands, toss the desiccated stems into the cup, scoop the fallen remnants from the floor. She stood up to find the dustpan but stopped when she remembered someone posting pictures on Pinterest that featured the garden of a woman who would, on occasion, manicure and plant her flower beds in such a way that the flowers, when in bloom, formed words. SMILE DEAR made out of marigolds for when her daughter came to visit after a particularly harsh round of chemo, BETTER THAN EVER with chrysanthemums for when her great nephew learned to walk on the carbon fiber legs for which he'd been fitted and they'd found a combination of PTSD meds that seemed to work. PURRRFECT on her cat's birthday.

Carly sat back down, started dividing the petals into smaller piles by color, trying to recall what her company's creative director had told her was the most appealing way to arrange primary colors when she'd helped him revamp the logo of a popular online handbag aggregator. She brainstormed, sketched an idea in her head, a slogan – take his flowers, make them yours. The design phase was tedious but she remained focused for the better part of the morning, ignoring intermittent phone spasms and the festering cold of the apartment, carefully placing the petals in alternating color and letter patterns and implementing severed pieces of stems when necessary. After several botched attempts, she finally got the arrangement right. She stood up and examined, impressed with her creativity. She took pictures with her phone from several angles, manipulating the shot she liked best with a filter that was supposed to make the image "lively, spritely and more saturated." She wasn't sure if that was quite right, but regardless, the work was done:

C-U-N-T

C-U-N-T   C-U-N-T

C-U-N-T   C-U-N-T   C-U-N-T

C-U-N-T   C-U-N-T

C-U-N-T

It was what you did.

She posted the picture on Instagram and got several likes in the first minute or so.

Picture Frame

1.

Cal says he's sorry for keeping you in that box for so long, knowing how dark and lonely it must have been. But you have to understand that Mrs. Warren hates it when he leaves, even if it's just to go down the street to the Dollar Tree. She's very unreasonable. If she knew he stole her keys and made the hole in her fence, there's no telling what she would do to both of you!

The important thing is that you are here in Cal's room now, safe with him. When he saw you tucked away on the shelf behind the shampoos and the decorative glassware, he could almost feel your sadness. A filthy shelf of low-end merchandise is no place for something so perfectly and beautifully made. He even took the time to wrap you up in two pieces of jaundiced newspaper and held you like a delicate child the entire walk home. He would have tried to find a bigger box, but he had to get back before Mrs. Warren woke up. She's always disagreeable after a long rest.

Cal thinks he'll place you high up on the wall facing north. Yes, just so. He's sorry to defile you with his clumsy hands. He will not touch you again. Now you can see the rest of Cal's room. He admits that it has seen better days. The wallpaper has started to brown and peel and his little bed table has faded in the sunlight. And that smell! The false hospital cleaner Mrs. Warren sprays when Cal is asleep to kill the cockroaches and remove the odors she says he creates. He cannot complain, though. The house is in a nice, quiet neighborhood that has been nice and quiet for as long as Cal can remember. And the rent is next to nothing.

That's Wife over there on the bed. She's still pretty for her age. If you are quiet and do exactly as Cal says, she may not even notice you. She sleeps most of the time. When she's not sleeping she stares at the growing crack on the ceiling. The crack grows every hour, just like Cal's love for you.

2.

Mrs. Warren is the fattest, ugliest woman Cal has ever known. She eats lard like air and bathes in gasoline. Her thinning hair smells of rabbit musk. The food she slides through the panel in his door is always wrapped in the morning's newspaper and resembles the crusty shrunken heads of cannibals. Cal gives half the food to Wife and throws the rest out the window. He takes the dull plastic forks that Mrs. Warren brings with his food and uses them to make a sculpture. He chews and files down the handles of the forks until they are sharp enough to cut, sharp enough to be of use. Cal wouldn't tell you this, but he's making the sculpture for you, to place it on the wall next to you when it's done. Not even Wife knows.

When it comes to Mrs. Warren, there are two things you must understand. One: be very quiet at all times. Mrs. Warren has feral ears, attuned to wavelengths not even Cal can detect. She lives downstairs in the Forbidden Room, but if you make even one squeak, she'll know. Before you could make another sound it would be too late. Two: never look her straight in the eye. Cal says that they are pitch black and fling shards of coal if you stare into them. That may not be true, but it's best not to take any chances.

Last night Cal had a dream. Mrs. Warren and an old man wearing a blue plastic jacket were standing over his bed. The old man held a blue box while Mrs. Warren spread paste on both sides of his head. The paste felt like a raw clam's insides. He couldn't move his arms to stop Mrs. Warren. She took two metal chords connected to the box and placed them in the paste, directly above Cal's temples. The old man turned a red knob on the box, and blasts of deep pink, orange, and magenta ignited the growing crack on the ceiling. Mrs. Warren's thinning hair turned into black fire that spread to the old man and to the newspapers on the floor. Then he woke up sweating in the darkness and heard Wife's snoring and saw her drooling face on the pillow next to him. Cal felt the wind rushing through the bars outside the window.

The next time you see Mrs. Warren and an old man standing by the bed, open your eyes quickly because it is only an elaborate illusion created by your brain. It is only a dream.

3.

Cal wouldn't tell you this, but the fork sculpture he's making for you is now almost two feet high. He's been hiding it under the bed where Wife will never look. In order to make the sculpture, he rips up old newspapers and chews the pieces until they are pulpy. He folds the wet pieces around the sharpened fork handles until the forks are sticky, too. Then he presses the forks together. Sometimes they don't stick together so Cal needs to chew more newspapers. So far the sculpture is comprised of five forks and almost four fully chewed-up newspapers. Just today, he chewed the entire Metro sections of two newspapers dated September 24, 2003 and December 1, 1997.

Sometimes Cal makes the sticky pieces of newspaper into balls and throws them against the east wall. It is nearly covered in spit and letters. Don't you think it looks better than the peeling brown wallpaper?

Cal hears Mrs. Warren's ugly feet stomping up the stairs. He hears the muffled clinking of glass and metal on his food tray. He must hide your sculpture quickly. If Mrs. Warren knew about it, everything would be ruined.

4.

Wife hasn't noticed you. At least she doesn't act like it – she's so stupid sometimes. Look at her red mouth, how it hangs open! Can you see the puddle of drool collecting on her chin? But still, she is Wife, so Cal must try to keep her happy. To keep Wife happy, Cal makes love to her every other afternoon. Sometimes she's asleep so he props her back against the headboard, pulls down the covers, and slowly moves back and forth until Wife is pleased.

But what he really wants to do is snap her plastic legs apart like a wishbone. He wants to thrust all the way through her, come out the other side (still thrusting) straight toward your wall. He imagines the two of you doing all sorts of similar things, which is silly, because we all know it would be impossible. But the idea of you doing these things is so alive in him, as alive as the cockroaches currently depositing their eggs in bean-shaped cases under the bed table.

Sometimes Cal thinks of you, of doing these sex things together, and looks at Wife. He feels ashamed. But he does not feel ashamed because of her. He feels ashamed because of you, because he knows he would be an inadequate partner for you, because he would never be able to fill you up the way he knows you must be filled.

When he feels ashamed, he feels horny, so he pulls off the bed sheets and turns Wife on her back. Can you see him whisper in her ears? He tells her he is horny. He licks her ears. Cal traces the wet lines around her mouth with his fingers. He looks at her eyes to make sure she hasn't seen you watching, but they are shut tight or staring up the growing crack in the ceiling, he cannot tell. Cal thrusts. Then he thrusts hard. The mattress springs and Wife's hips bend beneath the weight of his shame.

Downstairs in the Forbidden Room, Mrs. Warren wakes up. Cal hears her fat-stretched slippers on the creaking stairs. He hears her thick fists pounding on his door and a terrible scratching sound that must be her voice.

"Quiet in there! Go back to sleep!"

She cannot come and take you away from him. He will let her know:

"Fuck off witch!"

When Cal hears Mrs. Warren clomping back down the stairs to her own rotting section of the house, he is no longer horny. Instead, he takes two stained sheets of newspaper and rolls them up into a tube. He pushes Wife's drooping head off the bed table and moves it over a few feet. He leans down and whacks the cockroaches eight times. Eight hard whacks until he cannot tell the difference between their insides and outsides.

5.

Cal thinks Wife has left him. He doesn't see her anywhere. On the bed, under the bed, in the closet, over by the east wall. He's been searching all morning. She must have opened the window and climbed out. He cannot figure out how she managed to squeeze through the bars. Wife is tricky. Not smart, but very tricky.

She found out about you – it's the only reasonable explanation. Mrs. Warren wouldn't have been able to let Wife out. Cal still has her keys. Wife must have seen him looking at you while they were making love, or maybe she heard him speaking to you late at night when we thought she was asleep. Cal knew she would be jealous. His conversations with you offended her deeply.

It's not that Cal is angry, or even saddened by Wife's disappearance. She had begun to put on even more weight, beginning to rival Mrs. Warren. All she ever did was sleep over there on the bed. The only thing that bothers him is that when he feels ashamed, there will be no one to thrust into. You are too high up on the wall, the growing crack is still too small, and Mrs. Warren is far too disgusting.

6.

Have you ever had any madness in your family?

Cal only asks because this morning he was invited to breakfast downstairs. He wore his finest tee shirt and sprayed some aerosol mousse on his head for extra volume and shine.

At the bottom of the stairs a doctor waited for him. An old doctor he had never seen. Somehow, the doctor knew Cal's name and his occupation. His fingers felt like cold eels as he directed Cal into a tiny room, checked his pulse, tested his reflexes, cupped his testicles, and measured his cranium with a pair of metal forceps.

He began asking Cal questions. At first Cal started to fidget a little, because he thought the doctor would ask about you, about your affair, about Wife's leaving, but instead they ended up discussing irrelevant matters. He wanted to know if there was a history of mental imbalance in Cal's immediate family, if his parents or grandparents had suffered from any form of dementia, paranoia, schizophrenia, unipolar depression, and a dozen other big words Cal didn't completely understand. Which is absolutely ridiculous because, as Cal has explained many times, he comes from a good family, full of doctors and lawyers, leaders in the fields of engineering and politics. But he won't bore you with the details of their astonishing lives. He can see you want to hear more about his breakfast.

The old doctor had devised a way to shrink the nutrition found in a full meal down to the size of five tiny blue capsules. You must find that hard to believe, but it's true – just five blue capsules and a glass of water, equal in dietary strength to a plate of steaming hot eggs, bacon, grits and sausage. He passed Cal the meal on a plastic slab, assuring him it was as fresh as a newly disemboweled hen. His delicious breakfast was over in two gulps. He left a clean plate.

Cal complimented the old doctor's cooking, forgetting to tell him how much better it was than Mrs. Warren's gruel. He and his assistant, Thomas, were nice enough to escort Cal back to his room and tuck him into bed. Before they left, he fell into one of the most dreamless sleeps he'd had in years.

7.

Outside the window and just past the metal bars, a tiny honey-colored butterfly glides by Cal's face, then another. He wishes you could see them tumble together so beautifully. Puffs of air sometimes brush them against the grass as they move across the yard towards the fence. Then a real gust sweeps them up – five feet, ten feet, twenty feet – until they become two miniature globes in the sky. Cal squints to see them for another thirty or forty seconds until they disappear into a cloud, maybe the sun. Gone. Cal waits for them to come back, but after a few minutes he gives up looking and turns to stare at you.

They probably like it better out there, don't you think? Two butterflies and Wife.

8.

This morning Cal woke up early to work on your sculpture. It was almost complete. He wanted you to touch it. But when he reached under the bed, his hand found nothing except for three cockroaches swimming in a puddle of lint-fuzzed Cheez Whiz.

Cal tore apart the bed, flipped over the bed table, and kicked around some newspapers. He heard rustling downstairs in the Forbidden Room and thought of Mrs. Warren. Could she have seen the sculpture under his bed when she opened the panel in the door to slide him his breakfast? Had she found her keys? No, they were still in his right pajama pocket where he'd had them for weeks.

He sat on the bed for a few minutes trying to collect himself and figure out what could have happened. No thoughts came. Cal knew he had put the sculpture back under the bed after working on it the night before. No one else besides you had been in the room since.

Exhausted, he collapsed on Wife's pillow and turned his head toward the east wall. Then Cal saw it. A small piece of newspaper poking out from under the closet's door. He jumped out of bed, flung open the closet, and there it was, your sculpture lying undamaged on the ground.

Who could have done this? Mrs. Warren is too fat. Cal would have heard her huge feet tramping around the room. The old doctor is too pleasant. Was it Wife? She does hate you, and she's the only one tricky enough to slide through the bars. Like how she must have left Cal.

He has decided to hide the sculpture under Wife's pillow. That way, it will be right next to him at night. When Cal feels ashamed, it will be like he is sleeping with a part of you. Such a small part, though.

9.

Cal wakes up and hears conversations downstairs. He slides over the bed table and crouches to the ground, one ear to the floor. There are at least three people talking. The floor is thicker than he thought. Cal only understands a little of what they are saying but what he can make out clearly are the tones of voice being used. What awful tones! You may not believe him, but in those tones he hears the beginnings of a horrible plan. Cal is very perceptive.

It appears as though Wife has returned and is the ringleader. Cal hears the stupid squeals that must be her rotted voice. He listens to her tell the other people in the room awful lies about his treatment of her over the years, about Mrs. Warren's keys, about the sculpture, even about you! Of course Mrs. Warren agrees with her. She tells the others about how hard it has been to raise Cal by herself and to take care of him for many years, that it will no longer be possible to do so, that there is no money left to renovate the house. What terrible lies! Then the old doctor proposes something terrible. He wants to take you and the sculpture from Cal, to take him to a new house where Cal will be all alone, forever. Cal cannot hear the reactions of the other people in the Forbidden Room, but if they have already looked Mrs. Warren in the eyes (which seems probable), it is already too late. They are all brainwashed and tricky, just like Wife.

Cal walks over to the bed and lifts the sculpture. It is more than three feet long and the chewed ends of the forks are very sharp. He carries it into the closet and waits for Wife. She cannot find him here and if she does, he'll be ready.

If you love Cal as much as Cal loves you, then you will be very quiet. You will not make a sound until this is over.

10.

It has been twelve hours and Wife has not come. Cal leans against the wall of the closet as he cradles the sculpture, twisting it like a spit that drips with roasting meat. His silent breathing increases to hundreds of choked inhalations each minute. He turns his ears in all directions, just in case Wife decides to sneak back in through the window. She cannot surprise him this time.

Cal hears a noise downstairs. He grips the sculpture harder. Another minute of silence and then the sound of feet on the staircase. Not loud, stomping feet, but tiny, delicate feet, so soft that the stairs barely make a creak.

There is silence in the hallway. For a second Cal thinks the sounds on the staircase are only a dream until he hears the clink of metal on the other side of his door.

"Hey, you. It's time to have some dinner. If you eat everything like a good boy, I'll have a nice surprise for you."

Listen to her lies! It is Wife who would eat you both.

"I'm not fooling around. Come get your food or I'm throwing it out!"

Cal's stomach rumbles. Wife is tricky. But he does not move. He raises the sculpture and peels the newspaper back to reveal the sharpened forks. Though he is saddened by the destruction of his masterpiece, Cal knows this is no time for self-pity. This is a time for action. He forks until drops of sweat fall from his hands.

Wife pounds on the door. She pounds again. Louder. Cal hears a key scraping in the keyhole. She must have taken Mrs. Warren's keys from him and made copies when he wasn't looking. Maybe Mrs. Warren had an extra set this entire time! Still, Cal is well hidden.

The quiet feet enter his room. They walk towards the bed. The tray makes a soft thud as she sets it on the bed table. The floorboards creak as she bends down to check under the bed. There is no sound for a long time. Then the feet change their direction and come back towards the closet. There is a hand on the knob. It starts to turn.

"I know you're behind the door. Just come on out. We've played this game too many times already."

But this is a new game, Cal says to himself as he scrunches his eyes shut and kicks open the closet door, swinging the sculpture as if he were a madman. Wife screams and falls to the floor as the ends of two forks stab her chest, then her stomach.

The holes and slashes in Wife add up to all the times Cal felt ashamed. For each time he tried to thrust through her. For each time she drooled. That makes thirty-seven. Thirty-seven holes in drooling Wife.

Cal focuses his eyes and looks down, unable to speak.

That is not Wife's tray of disgusting food spilled across the floor. That is not Wife's scratching voice. That is not Wife's thinning black hair. Those are not Wife's failing black eyes.

11.

The blood won't clot.

Instead, it falls carelessly down Mrs. Warren's arms, chest, and stomach, collecting in the expanding puddle on the floor.

It looks more brown than red, don't you think? A nice shade of mahogany or copper.

Cal stares at her face. She is so fat that bulges of skin spill out from her sleeves, from the neck-hole in her blouse, and from under her filthy black stockings. Almost like the expanding puddle enveloping the floor, choking bread crusts, newspapers, cockroaches, and his feet.

It looks like syrup, Cal thinks. Maybe that's why he's stuck here. He cannot budge, not at the sight of the blood, or at the choking noises that soon turn to silence. The old doctor pleasantly shoves Cal away from Mrs. Warren's body, swearing loudly, pleading with him to tell him something, anything.

"Yes, I think I did it," Cal finally says. "And I'd do it again."

Before the old doctor can respond, Cal acquaints his wrinkled neck with the sharp ends of the forks.

12.

The bodies of Mrs. Warren and the old doctor become cold as all the blood slowly pours out of them. Their skin stiffens an hour after their ankles stop twitching. It turns a chalky light green. That's when the cockroaches and other insects become interested.

13.

Cal looks out the window past the bars and sees that the two butterflies have returned. It is a beautifully sunny morning. Their yellow wings are tiny matchbooks making trails of fire on the grass. The ruined sculpture rests on its side just below the window where it was dropped last night. It is more valuable to him now than ever.

There is no Mrs. Warren to bring food wrapped in newspapers on a metal tray. There is no old doctor to offer breakfasts of blue capsules. There is no Wife, not now or ever. There is nothing to help ease your feeling of shame. You must leave, the two of you, right away.

Cal will pull you off your wall, very gently, and wrap you in four pieces of newspaper. Then he will put you back in the box. Don't worry, you won't be in there for long. He will find a new room, one with freshly painted walls, a bigger window, a pleasant old doctor, and no Wife. He will place you lower on your new wall so you can be close and so you won't feel ashamed.

Neither of you will ever be alone again, I promise.

The Only Way This Can End

She keeps asking what he does even though it's obvious he's exhausted all of the permutations of the nouns and gerunds already listed on his profile, rehashing clipped versions of what he's already typed in their email exchanges. She says that the bucket of Coors Light bottles on the table between them makes her feel like she's in an interview ("Is there a clipboard in your hands I can't see?") so he moves next to her in the haggis-smelling dim of the Scottish sports bar, which looks like pretty much any other sports bar, that he chose because her social preferences included "low-key scenarios with a twist." At least here, just behind the open front doors rimmed with sharp-smelling cedar (he remembers carving wood like this into ninja stars at summer camp for an impending assault against a rival cabin that never came), he has a clear view of their respective vehicles – her moped with the duct-taped gas tank, his fixed-gear Schwinn – safely shackled together to a street light near the edge of the curb.

She gives him crap for leaving his phone on the table – "Expecting a text from tomorrow's hussy?" – even though it's laying screen-side-down, and who besides his great aunt has ever used the word hussy? She jokes about her helmet hair and the dirt-scuzzed Doc Martens with neon laces she uses for riding boots. "It's a good thing you decided against the tie," she says, "but I'm still not sure why you even considered it, Mr. Salmon Polo Shirt. I mean, we're not working now, are we? Do you want this to feel more like work?"

He'd obviously been kidding about wearing a tie.

The color of his shirt is coral, not salmon.

He wants to look at his phone.

He hears a finance bro at the adjacent booth tell his buddy to hurry up and buy the next round of three-dollar whiskey shots because happy hour's almost done. The idea of a handful of three-dollar whiskey shots bludgeoning his esophagus produces a sequence of satisfying images in his brain but she still has two-plus Coors Lights to finish and he's already used one bathroom excuse.

She asks him about his latest freelance projects —
is freedom from "commuter servitude" spiritually
and/or financially lucrative? For a second she reminds
him of a grunged-out version of Amelia, the petite,
plucky economics major who had been the first of a
handful of "serious" entanglements, at a time when he
didn't understand the inherent danger and stupidity of
attaching that adjective to anything. Before heading to
class years ago, Amelia would bitch about him sleeping
through mornings, warning about "misguided safety net-
ism," and who, from the pieces of social media detritus
he's glimpsed, had several years of mixed success in the
derivatives market before moving to Baltimore and
becoming pregnant/engaged to a mixed martial artist.

"I make it work," he says.

She asks about his gap year in Iceland, hiking
across glaciers, the thermal springs. His summers of golf
course maintenance ("I'm picturing a more angular
version of Bill Murray in Caddyshack?"), the type of bait
used to catch the striped bass he's holding in one of his
profile pictures, the seventh grade snowboarding
accident and subsequent nose job.

He doesn't ask about her life: the hostess gig in a neighborhood where the baristas have just begun to outnumber the crack dealers, why she still rides the moped if she's scared the engine bar will fall off, whether her own summer camp experience included the manufacture of projectiles. He assumes she wants to say something about herself, that her constant bullet points of inquiry are a cue.

She wants me to play the ancient game, he says to himself, shuddering a little at the childishness of the image, to throw the same stones she's been throwing. But he's already vomited up so many stones by spending years searching the bars for targets, that he has only two left – the ones lodged firmly between his legs.

He raises his hands as if to ward off a blow.

"I see what you're doing there," she says, shaking her head, her smile opening naturally. "Trying to get the check. Sneaky. Not going to let you give up that easy."

"No, it's cool, I was stretching. A little sore from the gym."

She tries to dig her thigh under his, asks him what his intentions are for the remainder of the night, as if she's giving him a choice.

A few minutes slip by and a graffiti-bleached truck parks outside the bar's delivery entrance. Several kitchen workers and the truck driver take turns unloading large boxes with the words "SPRING LAMB" printed on them, stacking piles against the building. One of the men mishandles a box, watches it explode against the pavement, a plastic-wrapped mass of frozen lumps. The driver mouths a curse.

He doesn't hear any of it.

There's only the animal in its pre-packaged state, sniffing idly at a pair of stainless steel doors, belly full and careless as it plods in the safety of the enclosure. A horn screeches and the doors open to a dimly lit corridor that smells of fresh-cut hay and something sweeter. Tagged ears lift, listen. The biggest male, trotting headlong and determined, hooves carving a trail in the dirt and shit. He disappears into the darkness and there's a noise that's loud but brief, then nothing. The rest of the herd pauses for a moment, then moves toward the corridor in a single wooly column, young, ignorant, invincible; unfamiliar with the sound of flesh ricocheting, ninja-star-quick, against thousands of tons of whirring metal.

An Occurrence at the Only Place You've Ever Known

Roger absorbed Allison's message, the acknowledgment of his cop-out deflating his confidence faster than the flushed, un-full dick that was still drooped sadly across his knuckles like an ulcer-prone salamander.

Drawing the blue alien thing and/or palm tree over it in the Snapchat he'd sent her had been a gamble, stupid enough for her to forgo an acronym and use proper punctuation in her Gchat response. He'd done it because Allison had told him about how she, before sending a pic, would sometimes doodle Pac-Man ghosts skirting across her cleavage, how she and her friends would turn their nipples into rabbit noses or penguin eyes or a "titmouse," her favorite pun.

Closing his eyes, Roger relived his thoughts and actions of the previous minutes, trying to figure out where he'd gone wrong. When he hadn't been able to find flattering lighting in his room or seated on the toilet, when he'd only managed to achieve the thin-blooded hard-on of a gun-shy flesh rookie, when he'd found it impossible, given the length of his arm, to get a proper dick selfie angle that wasn't an anatomy-book close-up but didn't provide too much unnecessary perspective, he'd decided to compromise. Life was compromise. A breast partially blocked by a stick-figure rendition of a woodland creature was still a breast. He could live with that.

He'd positioned himself at his desk, scrolled through a few of Allison's recent Facebook photos, worked himself to a state of semi-stiffness, gripped the base, extended his phone and tapped. The image had been fuzzy, the lack of contrast between skin and white tee shirt making for a less-than-enthusiastic representation of the focal appendage.

He'd used the app's drawing tool to make a blue outline, expanding its parameters, shading it in. He'd added green palm leaves and/or antennae on top of the head, and two eyes and/or coconuts about halfway down the shaft. Not bad, he'd thought. Open to interpretation.

There would be neither interpretation nor reciprocation from Allison.

- Full dick or get the fuck out.

- you racist against blue dicks?

- a little. come on roger.

- fine, fine.

Roger listened for distractions, hoping his suitemate might need to borrow laundry detergent or ask why the bottle of Lubriderm was missing from the bathroom. He glanced out his window to see if any of the likely green-card-less Asian guys working construction on the adjacent building were having one of their frequent smoke breaks-slash-bullshitting sessions, but the rooftop was empty except for plastic bags doing battle in the breeze. He remembered a movie where a maladjusted loner filmed a similar scene with a 90s camcorder and told his girlfriend that it was the most beautiful thing he'd ever witnessed. To Roger, the twirling sacks reminded him of a sadness he couldn't quite place, emptiness under the guise of total freedom.

More importantly, he had no excuses for Allison, whose emojis had gone from tongue-flicking and joyous to crying/barfing zombies.

Roger removed his boxers a second time.

*

She'd gotten his email from the bottom of an article he'd published on an obscure site curated by a former professor. Some drivel about the evolution of celebrity worship syndrome focusing on the potential illuminati symbolism of fingerless gloves worn by Beyoncé and Jay-Z at a diabetes fundraiser. She wrote to Roger that she liked his acknowledging that the "legal framework in post-racial America relies on the myth that racist concepts no longer exist," and was impressed with his portrayal of Beyoncé, noting that it reminded her of "that slutty girl who you keep around bc she's a hot mess, makes you feel better about your life and always has good stories bc she's a pathological liar – who i havent talked to after she got married at age 18 to a guy who needed a visa, just messaged me asking if she could use my email because she lost her pw. wut?"

He'd given up actual psychological research as an undergrad, and writing was a hobby in the downtime between preparing invoices and market analyses, but it felt cool to have a fan. Even if she didn't seem like the throws-panties-on-stage type. Even if she didn't seem like any type.

Allison Anvil. Her name sounded like a proto-feminist but retroactively offensive comic book character, like her online persona was administered by a psoriatic identity thief trolling in his basement for passwords and social security numbers.

Roger knew she was real, though. As in, not a dude.

Their exchanges followed a natural progression: Gchats, texts, following, friend requests. Her mobile uploads and posting history formed a more or less complete depiction of her last five years, too thorough to be forged. There were throwbacks of beach trips, a blurry ride on Disney World teacups. Diatribes about

Holocaust Remembrance Day and World of Warcraft. A Young Democrats dinner highlighted by a Bill Clinton handshake and an ex-boyfriend Roger he thought looked like a younger version of himself minus fifteen pounds of beer inflation. And the most recent ones — drinking simultaneously with lip-glossed companions from a bowl of neon-infused sludge, their duckfaces straw-induced and therefore permissible.

The kind of stuff Roger imagined he'd see and read from Jocelyn — the neighbor who did her laundry at the same time as him in their building's communal basement dungeon and, when she wasn't buried in her phone, appeared to be around the same age as Allison — if they'd been friends on Facebook or in reality.

Roger was a man who had done so much laundry.

He still lived in the first apartment he'd found on Craigslist, stayed put through several drug- and career-related roommate transitions and absurd rent increases, worked as a headhunter at the same IT company where he'd started even though he was mostly bored and there wasn't much chance for upward mobility. He used the same hair product — "power putty for a windblown surfer look!" – long after his faux-scraggle days had ceased.

In the nine years since he'd graduated and moved to New York, his only relationship had been brief and on FaceTime with a girl who was still at the school he'd gone to in Maryland, who couldn't deal with the distance between them and her desire for at least two members of the ultimate Frisbee team.

That someone who seemed to crave stability would remain single for so long was puzzling to the friends and coworkers who populated the periphery of Roger's life. He didn't suffer from a recurring skin condition or extraordinarily gross breath; he was no better and no worse than the majority of his boat-shoed, IPA-swilling comrades.

There were women, maybe one or two a month. Bar-hookups, Tinder dates, alumni functions. Connections that lasted a couple hours, or petered off after a few increasingly foggy mornings after, and ranged from the outrageous – the day trader who let him put it in her ass after he bought a $400 bottle of Grey Goose and told her his Kindle sales rivaled James Franco's, the daddy-funded poet from whom he received a period blood mustache and who later tried to cover it up by asking if he'd had a nosebleed – to the more pedestrian: a texting moratorium, an unrequited friend request.

It wasn't that he was incapable of reciprocating passion, that his moments of sensitivity were feigned and served an ulterior motive.

He was alone because, above all else, Roger loved ideas.

At age seven or eight, he would sit in Sunday school, listening to a watered-down version of Revelation, thrilled by the cartoon chaos it evoked. He would spend hours in his room creating his own action-figure End of Days – Mumm-Ra as the Antichrist, Princess Leia and Wonder Woman as angelic mediators, Ninja Turtles as the Four Horsemen. But a couple of years later, during a stretch of summer that included the demise of a second cousin, a cat, and a Siamese fighting fish, death became something far more brutal than the easy deus ex machina redemption found in dismembering a villain's plastic limbs. If there was a god, Roger no longer wanted to be a part of his or her utter fucked-up-ness.

Instead, he focused on another portal that was mostly reliable and seemingly infinite, where age/sex/location was as malleable as his grasp of geography and his desire to blend in with whatever chatty den of liars and pedophiles his clicks would lead him. His first girlfriend was ninety-eight percent instant messages and two percent hugs before and after school. When she broke up with him in-person before the seventh grade winter formal, using more audible words than she'd spoken to him in the past month, he was only shocked because her messages the previous evening had included the requisite number of extra vowels and punctuations – byebyeee talk to u sooooon!!!! – to make it seem like everything was going smoothly.

High school nights, holed up in a parental home office suckling on filched Bacardi, he would scroll through his AIM contacts. He devised and honed a system for gathering information, for establishing a connection that seemed more meaningful because it usually played out on his own terms, the rehearsed-yet-casual sequences of manipulation that belied the painfully ordinary insecurity that consumed his non-typing life. He'd start with a simple, hi, hey, hello, wait for the nm u? response. The trick was in dictating the movement, carving its direction. If KatyKay40286 complained about the frumpy patterns rimming her newly issued field hockey skirt, he would commiserate by mentioning how his swim coach had screwed up everyone's Speedo sizes – yea sucks its a little uh…tight hehe. After her expected LOLish response, he would write that it was probably nothing compared to the sports bras she was forced to endure (KatyKay40286 being a notable subject of bust-related speculation). Roger would then suggest that they play The Question Game. You had to alternate asking each other questions, one at a time, and that while the questions could be about anything, yes/no answers were discouraged. The game would start innocently enough – what life decisions caused Mr. Neary to become the kind of teacher whose coffee mug reeks of Kahlua every other class? – but would quickly veer toward the erotic:

> whats your favorite position?
> how big is/are your [   ]?

The questions were far tamer than what he'd encountered as a pubescent smut room devotee, but there was a thrill in the forging of textual intimacy, an arousal on par with what he imagined actual physical contact would elicit. If the girl got skittish and stopped playing or signed off, he would resort to another slightly less gratifying pastime: scouring the streaming video landscape in order to check in on which of his favorite starlets was farther along on the oft-tread arc, from casting couches and coy handjobs to triple penetration and rectal prolapse.

To an adult Roger, Allison was a welcome throwback to that indispensable era, though not in any sexual sense; the need to fulfill unrequited horny-boy urges no longer existed. Instead, they traded the facts – the loan-drowned reality of her recent graduation from a small school in a rust-colored Ohio city, his summer share on the straight part of Fire Island – and the obsessions – her resentment of a single-mother childhood and the sperm donation that led to her creation, his fear of developing colorectal cancer due to chronic Burger King gluttony – that comprised their inner and outer lives. She was fascinatingly ADD, filterless, able to jump in the space of a few lines from her internship at a law firm where she was trying hard not to perpetuate "America's meritocracy myth," to her quest to pillage the interwebs for the most awful sounding white baby names (my personal favorite so far is Kamdyn – aka murder capitol of the east coast), to the vitriol she posted on random people's walls: "You do realize that Native Americans are a marginalized ethnic group that still exist, not a cutesie halloween costume. and your baby isn't cute, fyi. is this an ad for birth control?"

For all she confessed, she never demanded the same from him. She could discuss how her roommate was a popular webcam model who got paid to play videogames in an elf costume and how sometimes Allison would try on the ears to not feel lonely, or how her bulimia phase had been so extreme that she wouldn't go to class unless she was guaranteed a seat by the door and a clear path to a bathroom, and Roger wouldn't feel compelled to tell her about how he cried constantly for months after he beat a pregnant squirrel to death with a nine iron or how he and his neighbor Timmy, before his mother found out about it, would take turns wiping themselves, post-toilet, as part of a game Timmy called "family time."

All he had to do was keep the conversation going.

He would come home from work or a bar or wake up late and activate one of his devices and know that in a moment he'd be inundated with the same pleasing stream of pathos:

ugh roggerrrrr im dying

i took a vicodin

but i just took it

whenever i get really bad insomnia i get scared that i've developed bipolar

because that's an early warning sign

and this is the age when people show their first symptoms

like stay awake for a week straight babbling like a homeless veteran

oh no. katy perry is back on Reddit.

save me from myself.

He could absorb her brand of damage until sated, take what he wanted and give back nothing.

Sounds awful :(gotta pick up a jacket at the dry cleaner. Later

*

After a year, Allison started trying to meet Roger in person. At first it was subtle. She was thinking of staying at a friend's in Hoboken, would he be around if they took the train into the city? She had to come in from her mother's house near Trenton to get her passport renewed at a Midtown office that happened to be near Roger's office, would he want to get smoothies?

His limp excuses – he was sick, he had to attend a company-mandated retreat at a mud-covered obstacle course upstate, he would be starting a juice cleanse that would render him unbearably flatulent – awoke in her a directness that Roger found difficult to combat. They could hang out on his schedule. What weekends did he have free? When was she going to finally meet the famous suitemate who used Febreze as body wash? She would have no problem sleeping on the couch as long as fewer than three sex offenders lived in his building.

Roger knew that it might go down like this, that she would try to sabotage the idea of herself he had worked so hard to cultivate and maintain. He wasn't skilled enough at Instagram to keep conjuring images of the places that coincided with his cop-outs, so he tried broaching the subject honestly.

- Do you ever think that if we met in person it would ruin our internet bond?

just that once you meet in person, that's it, it's no longer an internet friendship and there's no turning back and reinternetizing it.

Her middle-finger emojis were swift, relentless.

He was selfish. He was a solipsist. He was needy. He was too privileged to understand the consequences of cultural appropriation. He wore the same Third Eye Blind tee shirt in at least fifteen of his pictures.

Though Roger agreed with most of her accusations, he didn't feel the sting of her absence until the third day of signed-off silence. His coworkers had left their usual happy hour spot and he had secured a seventh pint. He was looking at a Buzzfeed list of horrible-sounding Trader Joe's products that "seem vegan but shockingly aren't!" and wanted to text Allison the link. He tried thinking of someone else whose opinion about the article he would find interesting or worthwhile. The bartender was mostly ignoring him, occasionally glancing at the dwindling pile of singles in front of his beer with increasing trepidation. With Allison he could drink to the point of being a dickhead and send her stupid shit and regardless of her response he would know that they were on the same wavelength for at least a few moments, feeding a deeper need, what he imagined it would be like to have someone worth coming home to.

Now he was simply another lonely dick.

When she signed back on (heyyy dummy I still h8t you and im never coming to nyc but hows ur week been??) he decided he would be more present, give a little more of himself, enough to keep her appeased.

Even if she only wanted to tell him about sending her ex-boyfriend Photoshopped pregnancy tests or her ideas about the patriarchy's relationship to anti-Semitism that evolved into a treatise on the shortcomings of biology. He would try.

if i could redesign sexy parts, balls would be on the inside, as would clits, and there would be no vagina, just a little hole, covered by the labia. and nobody would have hair.

it would be like the iOS 11 of genitalia. What do you think, rog?

- isnt that pretty much what a vag is

- no there's the other shit inside
i don't know what it's called
the labia minora!

- idk i kind of like my genitalia

- you're the only one.
the worst is when guys send dick pics.

like okay, i can tell if someone has a nice dick
but i don't need to see a picture of it.

-       note to self do not send dick pics
anymore

-       i'm not going to get off to a picture of an
erect penis

-       lol

-       you would never send a dick pic

-       haha only if asked

-       send me one
thats what snapchat was made for

-       i dont have an erection tho

-       that and me sending pictures of my
boobs with animal faces drawn on them
        how hard is it to get an erection? pun intended

-       very punny

-       now i'm inspired to send another boob
creature

-       do it

-       not to you. i would only send it to you in
exchange for a dick pic.
        i just sent my friend a boob puppy.

-       are you going to have me arrested if i
send one

-       no!

-       as long as you don't screenshot mine

-       i dont even know how to do that

He didn't know how, either, and wouldn't have done it if he did. He didn't want to deal with pissing her off again. The reference to a relative state of photographic permanence awoke in him a twinge of memory, an ugliness he tried to shake off while looking for his phone.

While Allison waited, faceless and soundless somewhere in New Jersey.

*

Roger took a second photo – this one blatant, unaltered – and pressed send.

As the image slid through the data channel to Allison's screen, he felt a sharp pressure on his throat, a sense of suffocation that sped down through his limbs, a putrefying heat. Then a dizziness like when he was a child and would intentionally spin in a circle until falling to the ground, except now he was trying not to move, fighting the downward plummet.

At some point his vision ceased and he was aware of nothing but a feeling of fullness, a widening, a roar of liquid forcing him towards an artery-choking torment. He was swimming in near-darkness, submerged in a milk-thick sludge that, while alternatively burning and sponging his lungs, was buoying him in the direction of a faint light that kept getting closer until he collided with an earthen hardness a few feet beneath the surface where the water was now soup-thin, gleaming. He reached for one of the root-like structures whose ends rippled and flickered from the embankment and it broke loose, rubbering down into the murk.

He reached for another, another until he gripped one that held, pulled himself and emerged into an air that convulsed, engulfing his chest. He crawled onto a sandy outcrop and closed his eyes.

When he opened them he was upright, walking on a path that reminded him of a condo-stunted nature preserve where he and other ambitious young degenerates would share saliva and hastily rolled joints. Except here the sun-doused vegetation pulsed with a velocity that made him giddy, growing denser as he whirled into what became a vortex, a sequence of spirals that disintegrated and regrouped as irregular rows of hulking columns, multi-shaded and huge and formed of

117

a substance that was softer than bark and free of branches.

Giant dicks. Thousands of them.

And tiny ones, lining both sides of the path, a sea-smelling undergrowth of brown and pink mushroom caps. The members implied an entire pulsing diaspora of masculine possibility: erections with varying degrees of height and curvature, throbbing and agitated, drooping, foreskinned willows, boulder-balls jostling the exposed earth, a coarse pubic lichen that could be dense or peach-sparse, leafy dark ringlets curling and twisting past the base of shafts, others manicured to a new-purse sheen.

As he took in the now-sharp environment, he realized that he had seen these dicks before, their context obvious in the memories with which they corresponded. Timmy's baby carrot dangling in a toilet bowl. His first timid side-glances at adult equipment (including his father's) in the piss-trough at the old Yankee Stadium. A fraternity brother whose primary career aspiration was to join an off-Broadway troupe of "genital origami" artists and who would practice his craft during chapter meetings. The ex-roommate he found one morning passed out naked on the couch, shit drooling onto the carpet, a sheet of bruised tinfoil splayed across his lap.

The path began to widen and bend, and as he followed its curve, he noticed that while the skin foliage was thinning out and revealing shards of waning sun, the individual dicks were becoming over-rigid and mammoth; redwoods where once had only been saplings. He easily recognized which porn actor each belonged to, remembering the many holes that had contained them. Billy Glide's barrel-girth, a ring of freckles just below the circumcision scar. The pale English hammer of Danny Dong, thinner at the base and rouge-tipped. And Lexington Steele, an obsidian tower stabbing and combining with the dusk, glossy with lube.

The path ended in another shock of color and vertigo and he found himself in a field at night, standing at the entrance to what looked like a medicine man's sweat lodge he'd seen set up at a "pow wow" near an Indian casino where his mother bought wolf-claw necklaces and he watched complacent men pound drums and yodel. The structure, under the clamor of

119

frozen stars, bubbled like a marshmallow, hissing from the pressure of whatever resided inside. The entrance was concealed by a curtain of six-foot-long chrome dicks, tips swaying a few inches from the muddy ground. He spread them apart, gently, and walked inside. As he tried to adjust his eyes and to not gag on the corrosive fog that now contained him, a groan flared from somewhere close and the hut expanded, recoiling at his presence. A spurt of flame – a hearth? – throbbed in a far-off distance and he moved toward it, coughing, lifting the crew neck of his tee shirt over his nose.

The smoke pulled and ebbed and spewed a montage of images, each featuring the same expanding and contracting protagonist. He saw himself in an earth-toned bathroom he barely recognized, his tiny pink nub sud-shielded and bobbing alongside rubber Sesame Street toys; slouching in a ski resort's communal shower, peach-fuzzed and shy-shrunken; adjusting to the unwelcome rawness of his first jock strap; cautiously assessing the welcome friction that resulted in his first unexpected dollop of salty release. An assortment of time-lapsed close-ups, varying levels of pubic hair, razor stubble, the sores last year that were only a harmless reaction to defective latex. And then, the twinge that had gnawed earlier when he'd sent the Snapchat to Allison: pictures he'd taken with a primitive digital camera and sent over AIM a decade ago – some full-body, others side-posed, spread-eagled – to someone named peachez00100 who never sent anything back, and who, he found out much later at a reunion from snickering classmates who had seen the pictures, turned out to be a guy he'd gone to high school with.

He let the old embarrassment rise and blind his brain with a shattering percussion that, when it subsided, left him cold and feverish, tongue swollen with thirst.

He was a few yards from the source of the hut's light, a tube of fire that loomed phallic and enormous, though it emitted no discernable heat. The flames in his direct line of vision parted and realigned as a projector screen that appeared to be operating at an archaically low definition. The video was a point-of-view shot, missionary position, the first girl he'd slept with – whose name he couldn't remember – her pleasure-stunned stares at him while he surveyed her neck, breasts, belly button, plunging in callow, arrhythmic excitement. Then a flicker and she changed, her body's outline blurring.

Lighter hair and lips, a thickening of thighs, paler skin, still familiar.

His dick remained.

The screen wasn't deficient, he realized. There were many screens layered against each another, a living composite of everyone he'd ever fucked. The length of time that each body would rise and dominate the surface appeared to correspond to how many times he'd been with that person and the duration of the encounter(s). The college-era girls cycled through at a brisk rate, the end results of mostly un-remembered brownouts or casualties of his prematurity. As the bodies beneath him aged and held their focus longer, it grew harder to look at them, though he had no choice but to absorb the emotions that manifested the same way every time: the pleading for something greater, a future not predicated on his dick, a future he would never give them.

After several minutes, he watched himself pull out and deposit a belly-smearing load, but instead of the relief and fade-to-black he expected, the girl/girls remained and he was still inside, though not in any way he'd felt before. He was the negative space that his dick had created, a shadow that nevertheless had the ability to bore beyond any untested womb, to inflict a greater pain that he now shared, the pain of never transcending a definition, of once-harmless ideas destroyed in a searing of flesh.

He knew what he was.

He tried to run from the flames and the screens that had separated and surrounded him in every direction, the lives he could no longer thwart, a white light and sparks and the stars were above and whirling and he leapt into it, screaming, and the light snuffed out and he was alone in a dim halogen glow and silence. Something soft in his hand and he knew without looking down that he was in the old recurring dream, the one where his dick had come off and he couldn't figure out why there was no blood and he forced himself to wake up but when he reached down he touched a smoothness, a nothing of skin, and he heard a humming laughter receding with the light, a joy from which he would forever be sundered unless he could reattach himself, if he could find a way to avert the stars' dissecting gaze, if he could convince his feet to move, if he could only…

Allison's message blinked at the bottom of the screen: nice, roger!! followed by a sequence of emojis that included various salutatory hand gestures and what looked like a frog with a potentially hazardous goiter. He reached for his phone, opened Snapchat to view the response picture she'd sent. One visible breast – large, pale, mostly unremarkable except for a nipple that was pinker than he'd imagined and possibly larger, if it hadn't been obstructed by the nostrils of a monochromatic alligator head. Ten seconds later it was gone.

Outside, on the adjacent rooftop, a hooting. Construction workers on their break, smoking, chugging Powerades. Most of them were lined up near the ledge, tossing junk from the vacant apartments they'd been renovating. Whenever one of them found something worthwhile – a scarred Blu-ray player, a pack of Parliament Lights – they would take turns aiming and dropping garbage bundles into the commercial dumpster positioned near the front of the building.

Whoever's bundle landed closest to the dumpster's center, Roger assumed, would win the prize.

One of the workers was cradling a filthy doll, clothed in the shreds of a baby blue dress and stockings. The head was missing an eye and most of its orange curls, and those that remained looked like they'd been burned. Each time someone hovered over the ledge, ready to toss, the man with the doll would move behind him and pretend to hump it, hold its arms and make it dance, simulate oral sex. The other workers would crack up and the tosser, also laughing, would turn around and smack the doll across the face or stomach, as if blaming it for his poor aim.

When everyone else had tossed, the man with the doll snatched one of the plastic bags that were swirling around the roof and placed his projectile inside. He gripped the bag by its handles, swung it in a series of circular arcs, and released. As the bundle flew upwards, doll and bag separated, terminating on the horizon, a black rift in the sun. A flutter of garments and for a second it looked like she might float down, saved by a parachute of fabric and air.

She fell no slower than the rest of the trash, made the same echoing crunch against the dumpster's metal.

The unencumbered bag drifted and landed where it had been thrown, where the workers stomped out butts, jostling and grinning, shuffling into the building through the fire exit.

Roger sat down and waited for whatever Allison was typing.

The Shelf

Rachel says she thinks there's a spider living on the underside of the shelf Patrick screwed into the wall above their bed. She says if she lies at just the right angle and looks up at the shelf she can see the spider hiding in one of the unpainted wood's darker knots, balled-up and plotting. She tells Patrick to come over from the futon where he's messing around on his laptop. She tells him to lie next to her at the same angle and look at the shelf.

"The shelf looks like a shelf," Patrick tells her.

Since the afternoon he went and bought the right size board and screws, he's noticed a rift between them, a rift that's become a tradition. Mornings, Rachel will say that the shelf and the books he's placed on it create too many crevices for arachnid romance, hives from which a brood will emerge with the intention of descending upon them in their sleep. He'll come home from work, greeted by the sounds of Rachel's sister's face talking to her through a tablet, something about "never acknowledging that coldness hurts," and, "Hon, you try too hard not to make a difference." Nights, he'll watch her as she straddles him, tits heaving like giant pale egg sacs ready to spill on his forehead as she scans the shelf for movement. They'll be out drinking with friends she's made at various points in her adolescent and professional lives and she'll make the same joke about not being able to finish a proposal by tomorrow due to arachnid-related organ failure and they'll laugh and look at him like a bruised thing that can't defend itself.

"I've never seen anything," Patrick always says, shrugging to make the laughter die.

Luckily, he always says to himself, everything dies.

He rolls over in bed next to Rachel, who's on her back, still looking up. She asks if he has an antidote for the venom and he tells her to go to sleep. He looks up at the shelf that looks like a shelf. He gets up and goes to the futon and opens his laptop to resume a game, to make sure his character avatar has enough experience points to join a rogue army that has embraced the demonic bloodlust of corrupt orcs.

"Babe," Rachel says.

"Go to sleep."

"Can you make me a glass of warm milk?"

"What are you, like eighty-five years old?"

"I read somewhere or saw on a movie or TV that if you get a spider bite you're supposed to drink a glass of warm milk or maybe pour it over the bite. Either way, make enough."

"I think that's for a snake bite."

"Can you please just make me a big glass?"

Patrick goes into the kitchen and pours some milk into a pan after checking the expiration date on the bottle. When he comes back into their room, holding the steamy glass with an oven mitt, Rachel is snoring.

He gets into bed, waits. The spider's legs splay as it web-bungees from its perch, closer to the bed than he can remember. He holds the glass above Rachel's head like it's a landing pad.

"You're not small and worthless," he tells it, encouraging, praying for some new violence.

Golden Age

Close to hyperventilation, you can mouth a few of the mantras you've developed until you find one that seems to work. "All of my electronic devices have abnormally long battery lives," you might repeat, lips scraping the pillow. Other lapses in composure require variations on the theme. "I'm a white man with a Nordic complexion living in a state with harsher than average gun laws. I have better medical coverage than the majority of nightlife industry workers. My frequent customer card at the local deli is one hole-punch away from a sandwich valued at up to $10. In the event of any significant hair loss, I've been told my head is nicely shaped and conducive to shaving." The talismans that, with varying degrees of success, hold back the dreams that are always about running.

At twenty-eight, you tell yourself in another black moment, your world is failing.

You're fucked.

But you've got to remember, you've always been a headcase. There were the night terrors that started at age four or five. The time when you puked Raisin Bran before school and for the next three months, automatic reflex, you woke up around dawn and started dry heaving, sometimes making it to the toilet but usually not, bile stains on the hallway rug, a routine that was squelched by a prescription for what you later found out, years later, was high-end Pepto-Bismol that tasted like red velvet cake. And relatives you see every three years still remind you about the time when you watched a news story about a girl who underwent a tracheotomy to remove a nickel she'd swallowed. You spent the next week choking yourself because you had just upgraded your piggy bank and something could have slipped and who knows?

You had to be sure.

Now it's summer and you've just gone on a fishing trip back in Connecticut because your old man's retiring and he wants to see you more. Late afternoon, you're sitting in the garage, shins covered in lake grime, cleaning the fish you caught and swatting flies away from your beers. You watch your old man examine your subpar work, the messy fillets that are plentiful of bones and skin fragments, the perfectly good chunks of flesh you accidentally flung into the blood-crusted bucket reserved for organ gunk and skeletal remains. You brace for another lecture about technique, but your old man stays quiet and places a fillet knife on the cutting board.

"When I'm gone," he says, "who's going to show your kids? I won't be here forever."

At night in your childhood bedroom in your parents' house, you look at yearbook pictures of someone you don't recognize.

Now you're choking yourself again, saying the mantras.

It doesn't take much.

When you return to the city where you live, you make an appointment with a shrink with an ethnically androgynous name whose mostly positive online reviews you've been tracking for months, even though you couldn't find any pictures of him/her, but you're cool with it because the office is one of only a few that take your out-of-pocket plan. You sign in with the doorman in the lobby of a 1970s-ish concrete abortion that looks like every downtown building, read headlines on the elevator flatscreen about a man falling sixty-five feet at a baseball game and the Dalai Lama's website inflicting viruses on its visitors. You get off on the correct floor where you assume there will be an office with a comfortable couch in a warmly dimmed setting, a Morgan Freeman type with the gravitas and wisdom of two centuries of psychoanalytic progress. After a few tense minutes sitting in a waiting room where everything – the furniture, the carpeting, the receptionist's hair – is composed of diverse shades of beige, you hear your name. You walk into a small room lit by hospital-like halogen lamps. Sitting in one of two chairs that straddle a large, tissue-box-accented coffee table isa mousey South Asian woman who can't be more than five or six years older than you.

"I'm Dr. K—," she says, standing up and extending a hand. "Have a seat and tell me what's going on."

The clinical florescence of the overhead light accentuates the shrink's mottled, child-scar complexion. Your chair is comfortable enough but you wouldn't want to watch TV in it. "I've been thinking a lot about dying," you say, getting right into it because you're on the clock, eyeing the tissues. "Actually it's pretty much all I've ever fixated on. Not really my own death. I think about my parents getting old, the elderly people I see limping alone down the street, fat kids snarfing Tropical Skittles and Doctor Pepper. I guess it's not that weird but for me it's like, palpable. I think I'm losing weight, circles under my eyes. My mother says they're hereditary but I never really noticed until recently."

"Are you religious?"

"No. Spiritual maybe. I don't know."

"This is something that people have been wrestling with since before the language existed to express it. The primordial question. There aren't any real answers, at least none I'm qualified to provide."

Morgan Freeman's voice wouldn't have made it sting any less.

"Morgan Freeman is a false god," you whisper to no one.

She asks you about your education, your hobbies, your sexual preferences. You imagine that each of your thoughts about death has contributed one mile-per-hour to the speed of a car you're driving on a road with a singular destination, a cliff of an unknown depth.

"You've got to try to stay in the moment," she says at the end of the session, "in the present, stay busy. If the negative thoughts start to creep in, think of something positive in your life. It's much more beneficial to be your own architect than to focus on things no one can control."

The pep talk is beyond hackneyed, but you've always been susceptible to encouragement. It's why you got good grades. When you leave the office and watch the video streaming in the elevator about a circus bear in Azerbaijan who has learned to ride a motorcycle, your hands stop shaking.

In terms of demographics, pigment, and the geography of your birth, you are lucky.

You stop smoking weed every day, lift free weights a few times a week, have coffee with friends you haven't seen in a while who you consider "optimistic" and not "coke-jaded." You initiate conversations with women at the restaurant where you're a manager and at the bars where you drink and these encounters are occasionally successful, i.e. frictional. You re-read the Eastern philosophy textbooks that you were drawn to as an undergrad and that now make the tattoos that say

"BE HERE NOW" in Sanskrit on your hip and the Chinese character the guy in the shop said means "Tao" on your back a little less like Phish-related mistakes and more like the fulfillment of a promise you made without knowing it. If everything exists in one moment, "before" might be irrelevant. Maybe there won't be an "after."

One night you burrow deep in a Wikipedia hole that ends with dozens of open tabs related either generally or explicitly to transhumanism, which, you read, is "a class of philosophies that seek to guide us towards a posthuman condition, including radical life extension to the point of biological immortality, fostering a respect for reason and science, a commitment to progress, and a valuing of human (or transhuman) existence in this life." The idea that you might, in the tangible future, be able to overcome physical limitations through radical technologies that are already being funded, to diffuse the death switch.

You love this shit.

"You crazy fuck," you say to yourself, giggling, but for the better part of a week you surge through websites that extol the possibilities of nanomedicine, mind uploading, postgenderism, cyborgization, artificial wombs, chemical brain preservation. You skim through the less interesting rebuttals from neo-Luddite haters bitching about the trivialization of human identity, hubris, coercive eugenicism, and dozens of other killjoy buzzwords.

Your parents are probably screwed, but you will still be middle aged in 2045, the estimated year of the Singularity, when things are supposed to really start going down, transcendentally speaking, when negligible senescence won't be limited to lobsters and jellyfish. You join Beta Race, an organization that publishes a monthly e-mag aimed "to deeply influence a new generation of thinkers who dare to envision humanity's next steps" and begin following the group's transhumanist lifestyle recommendations. You practice caloric restriction and supplement your mostly raw and vegan diet with up to fifty daily supplements that increase mental clarity, reduce cortisol release, and promote optimal health and energy in convenient, antioxidant-rich doses. Your coworkers start calling you PT, short for Purple Teeth, for the red wine you consume daily (one per meal and another after an acceptable cardio session) in order to maximize your resveratrol intake, and you ask them what you should wear at their funerals, when your Body Mass Index will still be at an optimal 18.5 to 20. They can't tell you to go fuck yourself because you're their manager but you know they want to. You couldn't care less about hurting the feelings of weaklings who have already given in to self-immolation. You learn to use group collaboration tools on your phone and visit personal networking sites to meet and communicate with other proto-posthumans. You download an app that turns your phone into a device to supplement your memories, constantly recording conversations and other audible events. You purchase better insurance that's more than you can realistically afford but ensures that the co-pay will be low enough for the regular examinations and blood tests you will have to undergo ad nauseum.

Your stomach might convulse sometimes at work or when you pass a pub, anticipating the succulence of animal fat, the release of hard liquor, but these are necessary casualties of the focus on everlasting survival, and denial is an essential quality for success in the cyborg nirvana you are destined to inhabit.

One afternoon you're jogging in a park on a trail that's almost the exact distance, if run every day, that will lower your blood pressure to an optimal level in only a few weeks. You avoid eye contact with the idle dying you pass – a liver-spot scarecrow reading a newspaper, a neck-lolling woman in a wheelchair, a trio of shagged-out kids smoking cloves, an otherwise hale-looking guy wearing a Ballpark Franks tee shirt thereby declaring his affinity for nitrate-induced gastrointestinal carnage. Close to a personal best time, you build up speed for the last few hundred yards, glancing at the occasional female runner heading in the opposite direction. One girl slows down as she passes, eyes wide, points at your midsection, sort of trying to hold back a laugh but also sort of concerned, and resumes her original pace. It's humid, you've sweated through your shirt and there are probably some serious swamp ass issues going on, but you are exercising outdoors during an abnormally warm autumn.

Water transfer isn't just normal, it's necessary.

"Uninformed bitch," you whisper.

You pull off your ear buds, turn to flag her down or at least pretend she's the reason you stopped and not because you're totally winded. You feel an unnatural squishing between your sock and cross trainer. You look down at the athletic shorts that were Carolina blue but are now crotch-covered in brownish stains, at the thin red stream that's coursing down your right leg, congealing, pooling under the tongue of your shoe.

An alert beeps and blinks on the activity tracker attached to your wrist. Your heart beats per minute have tripled.

*

Your grandmother had been afflicted by hemorrhoids for most of her later years, referring to them as her "piles." You'd always been careful to avoid the slime-capped Preparation H tubes and stool softener bottles that resided openly in her bathroom.

What's currently sticking out of your ass isn't like the gargantuan protrusions you'd seen in waking nightmares while listening to her graphic complaints, tiny enough to avoid the urge to seek immediate medical attention. Though that small relief does little to ease the throbbing that's making it impossible to sit down.

Curled on your side in bed, tablet-addled, you learn that fifty percent of Americans will suffer swollen veins in the anal canal at some point in their lives, usually after age thirty and usually due to the strain of soft bowel movements, constipation, obesity, or pregnancy. Though initially painful, the prognosis is rarely serious, and can usually be corrected by a combination of increased fiber, drinking more water, drinking less alcohol and caffeine, exercising frequently, and applying an over-the-counter ointment when necessary. Except you can't be certain that what you have is actually a hemorrhoid. You're too young, you don't drink coffee, you've been laying off the booze for the most part, and your diet has been endorsed after years of studies by Beta Race's team of board-certified nutritionists.

The bleeding might also be caused by a similarly shaped polyp, tumor, or abscess. You analyze the risk factors for each. Until recently and for as far back as you can remember, you've been a happy guzzler of red meats, processed cheeses, over-proof spirits. Roughly seventy percent of your penetrative experiences have been sans condom, meaning that HPV is more a certainty than a possibility. The human papillomavirus accounts for approximately ninety percent of anal cancer diagnoses, and the three dozen or so partners you can remember make this risk exponential.

Your activity tracker starts blinking. You remove it.

You look up Google reviews of the primary care physicians in your neighborhood. You're about to schedule an appointment when you remember hemorrhoidal Nana telling you in a brief moment of opiate-free clarity before she succumbed to the tumors that had spread to her marrow, to "never go to a doctor. I didn't for twenty-three years and it wasn't for lack of aches, there were plenty of those. It was because I knew, deep down, that the second they started prodding around they'd find something. You can't find anything if you don't look for it. Here I am, a few months past eighty, feeling okay, and I had the nerve to listen to your goddamn mother. A simple check-up. It'll take a load off everyone's minds, she says. Now look at me. Fucked.

Take Advil, get enough sleep, don't get married and you'll be fine."

She died two hours later.

You don't want to be fucked. You can't risk a hospital visit, allow yourself to share your grandmother's fate.

So you'll wait. Say the mantras, wait.

After a week or so your ass begins to feel better but one day you notice two identical lumps behind your ribs on both sides. Cancer already spreading from your lymph nodes? Maybe they aren't lumps, but areas of organ-related swelling. Early onset kidney failure is a possibility. You begin documenting the frequency of bathroom visitations, checking each urine deposit for color, opaqueness, bubbles, activating the stopwatch app on your phone to get an accurate measurement of its duration. You check your semen for blood and other potential abnormalities with the thoroughness of a tea-leaf reader, cupping it in your hands, sniffing. While pressing your fingers to your jugular to confirm suspicions of an abnormal heart rhythm, you press on something like a growth that clicks when you move it – a clear indication of a thyroid disorder that might lead to hyperactivity, irritability, memory problems, psychosis, and paranoia. A minor shoulder ache is an aneurysm in-waiting. You keep clicking the WebMD links. Sleep is occasionally possible, but only after the forced repetition of the glass-half-full self-talk that you haven't really believed in a long time. And an appropriately heavy dose of benzodiazepines.

After a steady, hazy string of Xanax-infused evenings, a new idea begins to take shape in your head, something different, something of which your grandmother might approve: you can't find anything if you don't look for it.

So you stop looking.

WebMD can fist itself.

You bury most of your electronic devices in your closet. You stop responding to what few texts you still get from long-estranged friends. Afternoons: bong rips, HBO, Thai lunch specials. Nights, you drink with a fervor. More often than not, your super, who also occasionally sells you Percocet and mushrooms, knocks on your door to tell you about the previous night, how he stopped you from flinging a slice of take-out pizza at a passing bicyclist after another sidewalk puke session outside your building. You give him money, change the channel. Mornings don't exist. Your cross trainers are ashtrays. You get all your shifts covered at the restaurant.

At least you're sleeping.

You're out alone one night and you meet a girl whose face you won't remember and who's almost as toasted as you are, but who sobers up fast a few hours later at your apartment when you ask her if she won't mind biting a mole off your back that you assume is malignant. You wake up alone in piss-heavy boxers, roll off the bed onto the floor, a howling emanating from your balloon-swollen abdomen.

Your time has come.

*

The clinic's waiting area is well-lit, featuring plush couches, a silent BBC news broadcast, an impressive selection of gender-neutral magazines. The only noise as you fill out your insurance information comes from the ambient nature sounds pumping from invisible speakers and a little kid making fun of his

145

brother for coloring an eagle green and orange in a book in the children's play area. A nurse enters from a side door and pronounces your name wrong. You take a last breath of willful ignorance and follow her into the examination room.

You don't remember the questions she asks you, and you don't remember your shorter answers.

She tells you to sit down, wraps a blood pressure machine around your arm and slips a thermometer under your tongue. "Ninety-eight-point-three," she says. "Very good." She frowns a little as the blood pressure machine relaxes from your arm. "BP's high."

"I'm always nervous," you say.

She nods, jots something on a clipboard, tells you to roll up your sleeve. You watch the plastic pouch expand with truth juice. The nurse divides the blood into vials with different color caps, slapping stickers on each. As she flicks her gloves into the hazardous waste bin, you imagine being sucked down with them, crushed against the loose needles and emptied piss cups, pierced and filth-bathed into a strangely melodic silence, a soft gray place where you have no concept of gravity and the squirm of your days.

The nurse tells you to strip, walks out of the room, not making eye contact.

The man who enters a few minutes later is tall, thick with the traces of what must have once been an impressive musculature, with an unassuming salt-and-pepper beard and a dignified hairline. He introduces himself with a deliberate, Julep-swilled drawl and a mitt-shake that's rigid but oddly pacifying. He motions for you to have a seat on the examination table and flips through the papers on the clipboard that the nurse gave him.

He looks up. "You decide to request all these tests yourself?" he asks. "Seems a little unnecessary for someone your age without a history of," he looks down at the clipboard, "anything."

But you know that's not how it works.

You know there has to be a first time.

"I've done a lot of research and, given my distinct set of possibilities, yes I need them."

The doctor shakes his head, reaches for a box of latex gloves in a nearby cabinet. "Well, all right then," he says. "Hopefully your insurance isn't going to murder you for this."

"I have better medical coverage than the majority of nightlife industry workers. I have –"

"Uh, ok. So which one of these possibilities will we be starting with?"

You guide the doctor's hands toward every abnormality and inflammation, watching for a glitch in his serene face, the flowering of concern, but nothing changes. He asks you to flip over and assume a position normally reserved for canine submissives so he can get a look at the scabbed-over flap whose throbbing existence can't be denied by even the most untrained eye.

"Yup, that's a real big one," the doctor says, almost chuckling. "This looks pretty straightforward, but I'm going to digitally examine your rectum for any irregularities, polyps, et cetera. This might be uncomfortable."

You realize he doesn't mean "digitally" in the technological sense.

You clench at the release of pressure and the snap of glove removal.

"Everything appears to be fine internally," the doctor says, marking something on the clipboard. "You're probably going to want to get the hemorrhoid removed for hygiene purposes. Shouldn't be too painful since it's mostly external. In the meantime, make sure you're eating vegetables and drinking lots of water. Easy on the alcohol."

The doctor tells you to put your clothes on. They'll have to wait for the blood work results, but all of your vitals seem well within the healthy range for someone your age, with the exception of your blood pressure, which he'll chalk up to a natural aversion to clinical settings. No need for a prescription.

"On a one-to-ten, how confident are you?" you ask. "I mean, I've read that misdiagnosis rates can be as high as forty-seven percent in a preliminary examination like this."

The doctor sighs, stares at the phone you've taken out of your pocket. "This is the golden age of hypochondria," he says. "You should get back into a more consistent workout routine and maybe find a couple hobbies that will keep you off WebMD. Make an appointment with a rectal surgeon to get that hemorrhoid removed. Otherwise, keep doing what you're doing."

You leave the office as you entered it, trailed by a rotting, skeletal version of your dead grandmother's face mouthing the word fucked on constant repeat. Three days later, sleeplessly camping on the couch amidst untouched plates of disintegrating drunken noodles, you get the call.

The bird-pitched, Mouseketeer twang belongs to someone who introduces herself as Holly from Clinical Imaging & Diagnostics who sounds like she's barely qualified to read lottery numbers, but at least she's bubbly. That might be the point. Syphilis with a smile!

"So, um, I'm going to read you the blood work results from your recent visit with Dr. E——? Please let me finish before you ask any questions, but honestly honey you're not going to freak. All the blood cell counts are great! Liver, thyroid, and kidney function are good…"

She reads off every result and she's right. You know because you've already checked what the numbers should be. She's "super jealous of your cholesterol?" and your STD panel is "totally negatory!"

You hang up, scoop solidified chunks of MSG into the garbage, and go into your room to find your cross trainers.

The next day you call your boss and tell him you won't be coming to the restaurant that night, or ever. You're going to look for a job where you can utilize your philosophy degree: arts conservatories, historical organizations, cultural think tanks. You run a little every morning because it feels good to be outside and moving. When you get tired you stop. You shave every day and dabble in some of the facial products that had been lying dormant on your dresser since before your thesis defense. You buy groceries at a store that doesn't sell kombucha or wild broccoli and supplement your non-organic vegetables with ground beef or boneless pork chops or whatever you feel like cooking. Your phone resides in closet purgatory when the retro flip model you purchased on Amazon arrives in the mail.

Whether everything is one big moment whose meaning shines perpetually or a collection of seconds adding to nothing, you don't care.

You're not fucked.

You're alive.

One afternoon you're getting ready for happy hour drinks with an environmental lawyer whose pictures are all taken from questionable angles and no full-body shots but who comes across in her profile as "relaxed" and "balanced." The phone rings, unknown number, but you're expecting a follow-up from the interview you had the day before for an archivist position at an online Nietzschean database. Or it might be the lawyer, XOXO-Jennie88, calling because she has to work late or something.

"Hello, is this J—?"

Monotone, rehearsed.

Telemarketer scum.

"Mm-hm?" Your thumb slides along your well-moisturized cheek toward the hang-up icon.

"J— this is Holly from Clinical Imaging & Diagnostics. I'm calling again in regards to some blood work you recently had done."

The twang is gone. The harmless questioning cadence replaced by stoic certainty, the weight of bad news.

Your thumb slides back, gripping.

You hear your grandmother's chalk-scraped cackling. You feel the soft gray place spiraling farther away into the bowels of a basket you'll never grasp.

"I'm glad I was able to reach you. I've been trying to get in touch for the past week but your inbox is full."

"Uh-huh."

"Well, I'd like to apologize for the inconvenience but there was a mix-up in the lab regarding the samples we received. An obviously undesirable administrative error. These things are rare but they do happen, and we make it our primary responsibility to notify those affected as quickly as possible. There's probably no need to be super concerned just yet – your cholesterol is still excellent – but there were minor incongruities in a few of the readings and we'd like you to make another appointment to draw more samples and to discuss with your primary care doctor the possibility of –"

"I have surprisingly good credit for someone my age and it increases with every punctual student loan payment I make."

"I'm sorry but that doesn't have anything to do with –"

"In the event of a natural disaster, my apartment is ideally situated along a major evacuation route."

"Um, congratulations?"

"I have three point five times as many Twitter followers as the global average. The footwear emporium on West Broadway is finally having its annual end-of-summer clearance next week and the mid-cut suede boots that match most of my collared shirts and a fair number of my jeans will be sixty to seventy percent lower than their current value. My cholesterol is still excellent…"

Either Way We're All Getting Eaten

"There's hardly any avocado in this and I asked for extra."

Jordan crossed his pseudo-stoned eyes, squinted between the half-chomped layers of the foot-long Subway Club sandwich he'd bought when they'd stopped to fuel up at the New England border.

"Aren't I supposed to have it my way? 'Have it your way.' That's what well-proportioned celebrity/athletes say on the commercials, right?"

"Probably most of the avocado is on your shirt," Ashley said, turning onto another nameless pastoral byway. "And I think it's 'Eat fresh.'"

Jordan giggled in the passenger seat. "Eat fresh," he repeated before taking another bite of his fit-for-human-consumption lunch. He turned his eyes down and started to pick at the green sludge that had congregated at the confluence of his salmon-colored button-down and khaki shorts. He looked like a decade-older version of the generically suburban kid from one of the more Adderall-progressive prep schools Ashley had met in Boston tailgating the concert of a band that billed themselves as purveyors of psychedelic bluegrass meets jazz fusion, whose obnoxious friends had called him "Jordie" and who'd made a weak attempt to sell her a sheet of acid that was clearly a strip of candy buttons. The only thing missing today was the hemp necklace containing a specific number of quartz healing crystals.

Jordan balanced the sandwich remains on the dashboard and started feeling around his gut. When he found the last avocado glob he grunted in victory and wiped it off on his seatbelt.

At some point he'd changed the Pandora to the Jam Bands Radio station. The antiquated grooves fell out of their windows and joined the rusty wind that had pursued them since they'd left the city, into a sky unshackled of buildings, leering in its vacancy.

She tried to focus on the farm-worried road and not Jordan's ash-kneed legs, which looked especially sallow against the black vinyl seats of the Kia she'd picked up from the carsharing service that morning. She'd picked the car up because today was her idea, orchestrated after she'd seen a subway ad for the service featuring a photo of a young couple embracing against the hood of a convertible, smiling amidst a pixilated sunset, the overlaid text reading, "No booty call shall go unanswered." In the two years since they'd randomly reconnected at a charity bartending event thrown by a mutual friend, something about a pop-up animal shelter, she and Jordan had been hanging out, at first casually and then tri-weekly, and it was cool. A show here and there, the subway ride with no transfers between their similar warehouse-to-loft neighborhoods: it was comfortable. Booty calls seldom went unanswered.

But they'd never ridden in a car together that wasn't a cab, she'd realized, never played bocce even though both of them claimed proficiency, never been to a beach that wasn't home to an overabundance of seedy Russians or the world's biggest hot dog eating contest. A day trip through sort-of-shared, once-recognizable locales might be a nice exhaling of the summer stink that had begun to permeate the city. There was some serious stuff to talk about later, but as far as Jordan was concerned, they would be zipping around, ironic-tourist-style, through rolling hills and second homes, en route to her ex-hippie aunt's cabin in a village named after slaughtered Native Americans for an early, locally sourced dinner.

Jordan had shrugged his consent to the excursion without even one smart-ass crack about cow-tipping, which was odd. When he'd jogged out of his apartment that morning minus the black denim he always favored, with the gung-ho of a too-old Homecoming drunk, shit had officially gotten weird. It wasn't just the clothes. His enthusiasm had stayed at a constant plateau the entire morning as he meticulously assumed DJ duties, chain-smoked joints on the parkway like they were going to a festival instead of toward retirees and mass dairy production, insisted on rest-stop fast food because "we must revert to a primitive state"—an energy she'd found annoying, then impossible. She had to focus on the drive.

Focus.

The road sloped down a lazy, gradual hill, ending at the first stoplight they'd seen in miles. Ahead stretched the major avenue of another small town neither of them knew the name of (Jordan had forbidden the use of GPS), but where she vaguely remembered years ago taking a shaky bike ride on her aunt's two-seater to purchase Nutella. They crawled past paint-chipped Victorians converted into chiropractors' offices, seasonal accounting firms, an L-shaped shopping center touting antiques, supplements, used Christian textbooks. A dandelion-laced green where a handful of sunscreened villagers—none between the ages of ten and fifty—lounged about on folding chairs or the grass. A trout-lipped shell of a former Stepford Wife was reading something on a tablet to a dazed boy in her lap. She laughed, flicked her finger across the screen.

The boy's jaw dangled, mannequin-slack.

Jordan put his arm out into the rush of air, undulating his open palm in slow waves. A pot-bellied dwarf with a caterpillar mustache operating a small produce stand waved back as they passed. His shirt was the same color as Jordan's.

"I could chill here," Jordan said. He dropped the empty Subway Club wrapper between his legs, licked his fingers.

Focus.

A pair of leash-less dogs sniffed and pawed at the gravel that constituted the parking lot of a roadside café. For a second she hoped one or both of them would wander close to the street, creating the opportunity for a collision that wouldn't be fatal but might serve as a means to rouse their tea-swilling owner from her crochet project.

But there would be no vehicular battery. She couldn't stomach the thought of adding one more stupid action to what had become an entire day of mistakes. The sluggish cruise through lawns of the semi-living, the dinner with a relative who, in the 1960s, had lost a dangerous amount of bone marrow from starving in solidarity with imprisoned farmers union organizers, who would probably get off on the farm-to-table app on Jordan's phone more than anything else, the misplaced expectation that removing themselves from their respective apartments might reinforce what she vaguely remembered from something someone had posted as a "shared ideal." The unassuming but meaningful way she was planning to mention the check-up last month that had led to the recommended appointment that had led to the pap smear that had led to the pelvic ultrasound that might lead to a series of significant and uncomfortable conversations in the immediate future and maybe for a long time.

She couldn't focus.

A live version of the Talking Heads' "Naïve Melody" came on, not by chance. She knew Jordan was mouthing as he hand-surfed to the beat. This must be the place.

"Could you change the music to the radio?" she asked. "Maybe NPR?"

Jordan pulled his arm in and fiddled around for a second, not changing the song, then ran his phone-free hand along the bareness of her leg, halting a short distance from the inseam of her cut-offs.

He told her to ease up on the pedal and that he'd just decided he wanted to get a dog, "like a burly-ass rescue mutt, you know, where it might be less than ideal to confine him to leash-walking and beating up on all the pug-rats at the dog park, but we could always rent a car and take him up here to run around for an afternoon, you know?"

"Have it your way," she said to the air in front of her lips.

It was June and that air reeked of lilies and bovine-produced shit.

She rolled up all the windows, jacked up the AC. She didn't glance over for Jordan's reaction. At the next intersection, she turned onto a wider road flanked by signs that looked like they might point to a real highway—the choke of fuel, the stomach-lurch of architecture, a digestive race through hard organs toward an afterlife with a face as blank as a smooth turd. She started singing along with the Talking Heads.

Porn with Condoms

At almost three in the afternoon, the subway platform beneath West 66th Street was slathered in the mid-spring drizzle that had been dumping on the city at an incessant clip for days, painting everything in shades of slop-brown and gray. That's how I imagine it: Marnie sitting on a doodle-scarred wooden bench, waiting for the 1 train to take her home, not paying attention to the rain-slick plastic containers leaking genetically modified dregs and mold dangerously close to her quasi-military boots – this was when she was still going for an "activism with an edge" look – the vinegar-mouthed MTA employee holding a mop and not doing anything with it and staring at her, the ubiquitous tired-ass old folks milling and slouching and wondering. She would re-read the text I'd sent her, try to suppress the start of what would become a full-blown smile, drop her phone in her tote bag and watch it land alongside her flats and the intentionally chosen manila folder that she'd brought to the interview, a receptacle as bland as the résumés and CVs contained within it, the doctored truths she hoped she would no longer have to rely on, at least for a little while.

Maybe she thought about tossing the folder across the tracks, letting the papers drift, precipitate, get crushed by the trains or chewed and shaped and used for structural support in one of Manhattan's abundant underground rat kingdoms, but she remembered the color-coded recycling bins in her building's lobby. She pulled the hood of her raincoat over her frizz-damp hair, closed her eyes and waited for the rumble and hiss of transit that now sounded like the start of a real transition.

I wouldn't see her in person until a few weeks later at the apartment of a girl who I'd met through one of the usual convoluted conduits of school/work/bars/someone-who-knows-someone-who-said-you-weren't-a-total-creeper and who had grown up with Marnie, who'd introduced the two of us when we'd moved to the city at around the same time a year earlier. Peggy, the girl, must have figured that living alongside two million people on a grid the size of an

Alaskan's backyard, it might be hard to make friends. From the texts we'd exchanged and the dozen or so times we'd gotten drunk together with mutual acquaintances, Marnie seemed legit, a little hard-shelled and wary at first, but ultimately crackable if you were the right kind of person with the wrong intentions.

And you liked marine mammals.

I brought Frank to Peggy's party. It started like every apartment party since the beginning of apartment parties: isolated islands of acquaintances slouched and close-talking, boozing and blunting away awkward vibes, trying to expand territory along the walls of the tiny white-walled living room and kitchen nook. Marnie was standing well beyond the coffee table demarcation line, talking to our host and sipping a microbrew. As she talked, she unconsciously tugged on a bare lobe that had been stripped of studs since she'd accepted the office gig at the nonprofit, her secondary choice of employment.

"Ayo, that hip little fee-male who keeps touching her ear and looking at us?" Frank observed, astutely, which meant they were going to fuck. This was before he moved in with me, when he was still commuting from his mom's basement on Long Island, when he was still, even though he belonged to the same vanilla-inducing career diaspora as most of us, dressing like a latter-day Fred Durst – Yankees fitted cap, dual earrings, XXL tee shirts featuring obscure skater-ish logos. But it was his thing and he owned it, slept on foreign beds far more than his own seminal-crusted twin mattress. Maybe he had an overabundance of the right pheromones, a huge schlong, or an inordinate percentage of the girls who had grown up on Total Request Live were still openly amenable to crude, pudgy appropriators of urban vernacular.

"Oh shit," he said, "here comes the baroness. You didn't tell me she'd be here. Led me into a goddamn trap, son. I'm going to find the bathroom. Good luck."

The baroness had arms that were covered in delicate translucent fluff, not unlike a malnourished Yeti pup. Her great uncle was the CEO of a regional commuter railroad in Southeastern Pennsylvania, which I guess was cool if you were into limiting carbon footprints or the inherent fellowship of shared transport. Frank had given her the nickname because, around the time of their initial penetrative liaison, he'd been reading

Wikipedia articles about nineteenth-century oligarchs and had convinced himself that her family's position within their chosen industry put her on par with the white-gloved progeny of an ancient American steel magnate. This imagined nobility also functioned as justification for occasionally waking up bare-assed in her condo after an in-case-of-emergency ending to an otherwise browned-out evening.

After all, one needed to keep his prospective dowry at a base level of contentment.

Before speaking to someone, the baroness would do this thing where she would trace the outline of her lips with her pointer finger and thumb and pinch them together at the bottom of her chin, like an old kung fu sage contemplatively stroking an invisible beard. On this occasion, even though it was past Memorial Day, the skin encasing her fingers (and the rest of her) remained untouched by the carnage of ultraviolet radiation, a virginal shade of cream. Which Frank might have found pleasantly appropriate given his flawed understanding of modern class structure, if he hadn't already taken up residence across the room where he was close-talking Marnie into something that resembled consent, opening a fresh beer for her with his keychain bottle opener that looked like a silver grenade.

But I don't want this to be about that party, how the baroness went through every possible iteration of what-does-Frank-see-in-her before beginning a mostly one-sided dialogue on the need to embrace the chaos of a universe we barely know or maybe just her desire to form a credible online persona (I was too busy following the arrow formed by her partially exposed clavicle, how it pointed to the couch on which Frank was discovering Marnie's earlobe with his tongue and she was looking into her beer and laughing shyly). How the baroness's ivory nails fused to my wrist and would guide me, more or less unobstructed, out of the apartment, into a cab, up an elevator manned by an interactive virtual concierge, into a shower featuring a showerhead with a pulsating massage setting (never told you about that one, did I, Frank?), and, much later, onto a sofa bed in a sun-bleached home office as punishment for the apparent nasal discord caused by my deviated septum.

How Marnie never looked up from her beer.

*

What I want is to go back, for a moment, to Marnie sitting on a bench on the 1 train platform, shielded under the rain-smeared streets, smiling at the text I'd just sent her. I can't remember the exact words I typed, something reassuring about how it wouldn't be the end of the world if she didn't get the grant-writing position at the ocean conservation organization, how lobbying to end dolphin hunting in Peru might be like viewing an otherwise arousing piece of obscene media where the performers were wearing protection, the fantasy irreversibly diluted by reminders of an uncomfortable truth, a shattering of ideals so to speak. The analogy's kind of a stupid one, I know, but I like to think she got it.

Frank wouldn't be able to tell you this, lurking squalid in the outer-borough hovel of whoever's fucked up enough to keep listening to his resin-mouthed lamentations, but Marnie had always wanted to be a cetologist, until she accepted that her lack of proficiency in mathematics and her debilitating fear of defaulting on more student loans meant that several years in a graduate program studying whales and dolphins was an impossibility. The passion was still there, though, strong as ever. She could close her eyes, lean back in one of the patio folding chairs Frank brought with him when he moved in with me, and describe the cunning subterfuge involved in the group mating practices of porpoises or the peach-fuzzy nuzzle of a manatee calf's flipper with the trancelike cadence of an artist or a monk, trying to reproduce the drama within herself, punctuating her verbal reveries with a guttural sigh that was far more sensual than anything I ever heard beyond the ramshackle wall that separated my room from Frank's.

She could transport you to places untouched by the shoreline's chem-trail and fluoride-tinged sprawl, make you feel like you were totally submerged, a not-quite-initiated interloper absorbing the contours of reefs and the warm modulation of transoceanic currents rather than the corroding jigsaw of fire escapes and tobacco dregs that comprised the view beyond our apartment's back window; the hulking shadows above us were no longer cast by a precarious water tower whose ladder Frank had often suggested climbing if we were sufficiently tripping our faces off, but by the smooth, intimidating girth of a blue whale's underbelly as it breached the surface.

I wonder, when she finally got on the train that afternoon after her failed interview, what aquatic imagery she decided to drape over the rust and plastic confines of the car. Did she see, on the seat next to her, a fortysomething snub-nosed woman in hospital scrubs playing Candy Crush or a fixated otter floating on its back, manipulating a freshly caught sea urchin with its paws? Was the too-young mother across the aisle angrily shoving her hyper toddler back into his stroller or simply shielding her calf from famished polar bears with a pale beluga fin? Did the lock-jawed leather-skin, shoeless and snoring on the handicapped-accessible bench away from the other passengers, transform into an aged bull walrus writhing in beach-scented grime after his final defeat?

I keep going back to those moments, even though I wasn't there, even though I can't pretend to have any true understanding of what she was seeing, even though nothing I've described might have actually happened. Not that it matters. Because for me, Marnie on the subway will always represent an embodiment, not of that year, but of that year's potential, unvarnished by the summer and everything that came after.

And what did come after?

Humid happy hours at that one rooftop bar we liked, brain-frozen on slushy margaritas, Frank's sexualized eye appraising the server's floral skirt or yoga pants while Marnie would suggest that we could take the city's money by jumping from a certain height onto (and through) the subway grates. Later, high and giggling, we would listen to the elderly clarinetist a couple floors above us and claim we could do better before jacking up one of Modest Mouse's early albums and readying our addled bloodstreams for another round. Mornings, the floor jolted and the windows shook and a smell of burning would fill the air in Frank's room until the two of them groggily emerged. Except for the time it was just her, covering her drooping mouth and bee-lining to the bathroom where she stayed for the better part of the next two days.

Breakfasts were a suburban memory.

Sometimes Marnie would start shivering, even in the heat, and Frank would hold her with a metallic aftertaste on his lips. Cabs were rare and there were never stars. One night, standing on the sidewalk where the gum stains speckled the pavement like spots on a robin's egg, she asked us to lie beside her, to watch the synthetic-orange night and the endless space behind it. Frank looked up from something on his phone, smirking, and asked if we'd known a lot of Jews in high school.

There were weeks when none of us slept.

When it started to get really bad, after she'd gotten fired and Frank started spending every third night at the baroness', I began to believe that Marnie had psychic powers, that she could predict the future. She told me Frank was the worst man in her life who wasn't really the man in her life and would remain the worst for a long time. That this world, ruled by parents who knew for sure that their God agreed with them, was not and would never be a safe place for children. She would describe apartments she hadn't moved into yet, the progress of next year's impending nor'easter.

She took to sleeping in my bed, the window open, always smelling like salty flowers no matter how long it had been since she'd washed or eaten. When she was lucid enough, I'd read to her from the marine ecology book slash personal memoir – "The Bottlenoses of Biscayne Bay" by Dr. J.R. Mazza – that Frank had stolen from an unlocked U-Haul the morning after they'd met, until she drifted off into the wet, blue world only she could touch. Maybe she'd already been there the whole time, from that day on the subway right until the end, the brilliant mid-October afternoon when her big linebacker cousin with the sorrowful expression and neon track shoes came to carry her out to the car where her sunglassed parents were waiting and Frank tried to lash out at him, halfheartedly, and Marnie just sat there on the futon looking at us, cold and unblinking, frozen, immersed in the facts I'd been reciting from the pages she'd already memorized, the facts she would always know better than any of us pathetic dry-landers.

In captivity, dolphins have lived as long as forty years. In the wild, though, scientists believe they only live twenty-five to thirty years.

Some specific whistles, called signaling whistles, are used by dolphins to identify and call each other, and besides immediate family members, imitation of the signature whistle seems to occur only among befriended adult males.

A bottlenose's skin feels like rubber due to an absence of any sweat glands and an unusually thick epidermis, ten to twenty times thicker than that of other terrestrial mammals. The skin will peel and flake off in order for new skin cells to replace the older ones. This is similar to how human skin cells are replaced. The layer under the epidermis is where the nerves, connective tissues, and the blood vessels are found.

If a dolphin's tooth gets knocked out, it's never replaced.

Dams

She walks down the path that leads from the main building to the stream that runs parallel with the clinic and staff bungalows, a splice of indigo heading southeast through the cloud-hung mountains toward Walmart country. It's late September and warm, but she can smell wood smoke coming down from the ridge that marks the border with either Tennessee or Kentucky, maybe both. She can't remember.

She scans the bank for towels left by housemates or counselors, walks to the end of the rickety dock, kneels on the bare wood, and listens.

Bird banter, nothing else.

She dips her hands, ink-smudged from the paperwork she's been filling out, and watches the current slow through her fingers, then quicken where the stream bisects a sandbar and disappears around a stone-lined bend. She glances back down at her reflection in the water. It's a trick she's been saving since the afternoon last week when she started the application to begin outpatient therapy.

If she catches herself from the right angle and with just the right amount of distortion from the ripples, the stream might show her something new, something she might want to look at.

*

When she's ten or eleven, her father's brother and his family come to visit, the only time she can remember meeting them. They've been traveling through coastal suburbs in their crummy minivan on what her uncle calls "field service," which seems to consist of handing out poorly photocopied booklets with a lighthouse on the cover to mostly indifferent and occasionally aggressive strangers. Her parents keep a stack of the booklets they've been mailed over the years in the garage for when it's raining or snowing and the dogs need to be wiped down.

This is Uncle Randall and brood's last pit stop before returning home to a village somewhere near Canada that her father refers to as Cultsville, USA, which causes her mother to snort out sangria if it's late enough in the afternoon.

Everyone's sitting on the back deck sipping iced tea except for her parents and her father is fiddling with a cigarillo he hasn't lit yet. Her cousin Darryl, a few years older and more worm-necked than the pictures she's seen of him, has been staring at her since exiting the rust-scarred Dodge Caravan, sullen and not saying anything. She thinks he might have an embarrassing speech impediment or maybe teenagers in Cultsville aren't allowed to talk, until he turns to her aunt and whispers, loud enough to hear, "She's going to be a dyke, isn't she?"

Her uncle tugs at the edge of a thicker version of the lighthouse booklet in his stick-figure lap, looking in the direction of the driveway. Her aunt, red-faced and full with fetus, starts sputtering until her father cuts her off.

"You never know, the kid may be right," he says, wheezing out a smoker's giggle. "That's the first rational observation I've heard today. You should let him take the lead on your next pilgrimage or whatever."

After her relatives leave, she searches for "dyke" in the CD-ROM encyclopedia on her desktop. From the Dutch: a dirt-made embankment that regulates water levels. She's showered recently and her parents are Serbian and Irish. She isn't tall, fat, or barricade-like. Darryl, she assumes, is just bitter because he has to wear tucked-in Goodwill polos and black Velcro sneakers that contribute to an existence plentiful of schoolyard beatdowns (in a town where people still say "schoolyard"), if he isn't homeschooled.

She watches herself brush her pixie-chopped hair in the bathroom mirror, black-polished fingernails smoothing the tides of frizz like inverse moons. The boys in her class always compliment her thrift store flannels and the Nirvana tee shirt featuring a squiggle-mouthed smiley face with Xed-out eyes that she wears biweekly and is wearing now despite being unfamiliar with most of the band's oeuvre besides a dubbed cassette of the acoustic album. And the girls, though she knows they'd never admit it, gawk at her hands and wish their mothers were pill-despondent or hungover enough to let them out of the house in anything but their mall-bought, middle-school-bland sweaters and skirts that never seem to hug tight enough.

Maybe Darryl has a point.

She likes to control the flow.

A couple years later the internet – and an unintentionally hilarious dude with Tourette's in her biology lab – teaches her alternate definitions of words that aren't in her encyclopedia, definitions you don't want to carry around as an appendage. She would keep her black nails but construct her own version of an acceptable archetype, not quite another pre-melanoma Abercrombie princess but close enough to silence her father and the guys who don't listen to Nirvana and who consider a fifth of Mad Dog, a bottle of Sprite, and a post-party ride in a bass-riddled Yukon Denali as appropriate currency for a half-remembered skin-prying.

Nights splayed across SUV back seats are fine, as long as the buzz is adequate, but she admits long before her first semester at a small "nonjudgmental" college in her metropolitan area's largest city that her cousin was probably right, regardless of his intended definition. She beds flat-chested and septum-pierced Caroline during Orientation Week (a source of endless bad puns), then a couple of rugby butches, a theater hipster who identifies herself as "pan-curious," the klepto with the Hoover-mouth from Georgia who cries about her missionary fiancé in Yemen, Caroline again.

Then the year of the Ex that starts with a hash-oil vaporizer at 3am outside of IHOP and ends in volcanic shards and a couple hundred dollars of pawned electronics.

A week or so after the breakup, the bearded, sag-jawed bartender she's been crashing with for the past three nights mentions her nails. Still painted the same way, automatic reflex, taken for granted and absorbed into the rest of the mess.

"Ten mini black daggers harvesting my essence," he jokes, pointing at his chest, at the welts she doesn't remember making.

He's using a health insurance card to combine crushed Adderall pills and the coke he says is mostly speed and baby powder, creating "generational hybrids." Sitting on the edge of his bed, feeling the sinus heat from the first session, she braces for a punch line that never comes. Instead, he hums along to the 80s synth pop playlist – titled "The Decade(nce) That Never Dies"

– pulsing from his desktop, swivels in his office chair, picks her up and positions her in his lap, in front of the glass slab where he's been chopping.

When she wakes up she's back in bed on her side and he's pecking at the space behind her earlobe. Rubbing his half-boner against her knee. She pulls away, buries her face into the duvet cover.

"It's okay," he's saying, rubbing, "you're okay. You stuffed your fist into your mouth and were like choking or gnawing on your fingers or something. Once I saw that you weren't having a seizure I assumed you just needed to relax. You were sleeping. I helped."

"Did you finish all the lines?"

She tells herself to find nail polish remover.

*

Reeling, bloodshot, she flings Kandi's miniskirt and bra at the detritus that's partially blocking their shared toilet, a compost of night sweat and perfumed smudge that might fester intact until the end of the semester. Her roommate's sty of a life (another Ex-ism) is only redeemed by her innate ability not to notice anything.

She opens her window to let in a wash of air, to let out the lingering odor of charred rubber.

*

The goodbye – expectedly stiff, quick and almost wordless.

The Ex uses a copied key to enter her dorm room without knocking, without giving her enough time to hide the baggies. She hops on the futon, the plastic fusing to the side of her be-thonged ass and thigh.

She wants it to be like the beginning when The Ex would burst in Kramer-style while she was reading and they would bullshit about mutual friends, overdraft fees, The Pixies, lucid dreams. Or they'd make out a little, and before they fell asleep The Ex would do her best George Clooney, Good night, and...good luck...

"You look like fucking garbage," The Ex says, sniffing the room, dead-voiced. "I heard you were at O'Connell's last Friday. Jason said you were buying shots and left with an older guy with a weird scar on his neck or something."

She wants to remind The Ex about the nights they'd philosophized about what they would be doing and where they would be in a few years. Freelancers, institutional mules, ski lodge waitresses. She would forge college admission essays for clients she would find on Craigslist. The Ex would manage a sperm bank. There would be deadlines, alumni events, memorials to attend, vibrators, clubs, nipple slips, and brunches. And later, probiotic baby food, Hers and Hers bidets, nurses at four in the morning.

"Would you like some spah-kaling water?" she says, the inside joke falling flat before it exits her bark-thin lips.

The Ex walks toward her, lifts her face with cupped hands. Her eyeliner-tears slide down the Ex's forearms, forming inky tributaries at the elbows. The Ex brushes the salty blackness off before it reaches her prized Pearl Jam tee shirt and steps back, nearly tripping over some of Kandi's ranker thongs and a couple tampon wrappers.

She wants to talk about the last few months. She doesn't.

"You owe me a watch and an iPad," The Ex says. "I don't give a shit about the earbuds, I'd be surprised you were even able to get anything for them." She starts walking toward the hallway.

"When?"

"Whenever. You have my PayPal. Oh, and I'm transferring."

"When?"

The Ex shuts the door behind her.

She reaches for the baggies that have been exposed the entire time and feels the coolness of a glass stem.

*

After lunch and before Cognitive Behavioral Education, she sits in a folding chair on a vine-walled patio next to a small patch of legumes and vegetables she helps tend, smoking Marlboros with Eric and Dave.

Eric is in his mid-to-late-twenties, pudgy and rosacea-flushed, generic side-swept hair and blue cardigan, Northeastern non-accent, never makes eye contact.

Dave is beef-bellied, self-proclaimed "OG roughneck" who looks like he probably sported several different goatie/rat-tail combinations in the early- to mid-nineties, and who, she thinks, would probably be attractive to someone looking to get thrown around a little.

They're sitting around a small circular table, staring at the garden.

"The string beans are doing OK, but those tomatoes are getting huge," Eric says, ashing onto his lap. "They're like…"

"Goat balls right!" Dave says.

"How do you know what goat balls look like?"

"You think because I'm from Queens I never seen a goat?"

"No, I –"

"Well you're right, I hadn't. Up close. Until the drive down here. Me and the lady stopped at this farm because she wanted to buy vegan lip balm or some shit and I walked around to this pen where they had ducks and chickens and donkeys and these mini-llama things, uh…"

"Alpacas?"

"Fuck if I know. Anyways in the corner is this big goat, looks like he's sitting on a boulder but when he gets up, blam! Dude's got some real low-hangers, like I for real thought it was some kind of freak midget cow haha but nah there were two balls and I'm looking around for a chick goat because I'm like this guy has to get laid ay-sap, those things were like dragging on the dirt, all red and scuffed, just like your tomatoes over there."

"I wish you didn't have to be so gross," Eric mumbles, reaching for the communal pack. Dave snatches it away, removes the last cigarette, balls the pack in his fist and lets it fall onto the patio's brick tiles.

"I call it like I see it dude. Baby girl gets it, am I right?"

"I think they look more like my parents' Rottweiler's," she says, "before he got neutered."

"Ha! See? You need to lighten up."

Eric reaches for the largest cigarette butt in the ashtray at the center of the table, tries to smooth it out.

"I need to stop setting unrealistic expectations and become less ambivalent about my recovery."

"Man stop repeating these counselors and doctors. What you need is what the goat needs. Some pussy. Or at least the prospect of pussy. Sorry baby girl."

She shrugs, inhales the last of her smoke.

"Sexual contact between residents is explicitly prohibited and may result in immediate dismissal. Which, for me, would mean breaching a court order. Which would..." Eric grabs his left hand with his right hand to stop them both from shaking.

"Bro," Dave says, "I'm not saying hook up with someone here. Baby girl's not your type – and honestly out of your range – and the rest of these motherfuckers are basically comatose and like –"

"Mentally broken? Unable to experience pleasure?"

"I was going to say like introverted but that's not right."

"Isolated," she says.

"Isolated. That's what's up. Nobody with twenty-five percent of their head screwed on would want to be put in isolation upstate, but here they look for it. No, you want someone immune to your particular brand of bullshit, like my lady, someone you can talk to on a real level, someone who can calm you down, stop you from doing something stupid. Also: pussy. How you think I stay so jolly? It's not from being all Johnny green-thumb every day, that's for sure. I never see you make any calls to anyone when they let us."

Eric starts rocking and hugging himself and she knows what's coming next. She turns away from the table and scans the garden for signs of the Brussels sprouts she planted a few months ago finally forcing themselves out of the earth.

"There is someone I let myself think about sometimes," Eric says. "An account manager where I used to work. We were put on the same project right before I had to leave. She had really big green eyes. Like leaves or something. She seemed really, um, clean."

"Call her then."

"I can't."

"You scared?"

"No, I mean yeah, I mean the quickest way I'd be able to find her number or email is on Facebook or LinkedIn but I had to deactivate them after the restraining orders and even if I created a new account and friended her there's an overwhelming probability that the counselors will contact my probation officer and then, you know, can't risk it."

Dave finishes his cigarette, flicks it like a paper football between two wooden string bean poles. "All I know is I'm pretty sure it's hard to get locked up for talking shit to someone on a computer. Not even talking shit. You were basically just repeating stuff that actually happened."

"Not just repeating," Eric mutters, twitching again, searching his pockets for something that isn't there. He sighs/groans. "I'm fucked."

Even though it's her favorite time of day, when the sun seems to hover, to taste the day's evaporating embers before beginning what she once described as a "violent downward purge" in a free-write session, she considers leaving the patio and sitting in her room until dinner.

She's heard the build-up to Eric's demise, all of the variations that depend on his current intake of anti-psychotics. The post-college slump year that turned into a decade. The beers that turned into shots that turned into coconut water that turned into crushed Dexedrine that turned into Valium and high fructose corn syrup. The anxiety, the skin issues, the gastrointestinal issues, the money. The lack. The profiles of lives that had once intersected with his, getting older like he was but full. Their promotions, masters programs, the moves from studios to one-bedrooms to first mortgages, the second and third long-term relationships, engagement updates, the baby/puppy/vacation, the waking up early on weekends, farmers markets, nostalgic three-day hangovers, the passively self-congratulatory links to articles – 25 Things You're Too Old for When You're 25 – the faux-existential uproar.

Mostly he would focus on a selection of the women he'd known. Single-night randoms, sharers of a few dates, girlfriends of a few months. Buoyed by an aching OxyContin lull, he would obsess over the details of their departures from his life, deciding that in most cases it hadn't been entirely his fault. They'd been immature and incapable of knowing what they wanted or needed. They hadn't given him enough time to reach his potential as a lover. They were the unwitting products of a second or third-generation throwaway culture.

He would study the men who populated the pictures they posted, gauging the possibility of intimacy until it was obvious. He tried to make himself angry at these beneficiaries of his sloppy seconds, but didn't they have a right to know what their girlfriends and fiancées had done with him not so long ago, what they were capable of? He would have wanted someone to tell him.

The first messages he sent were basic; a clinical description of a specific encounter – …underwear discard (both), digital stimulation (her), missionary penetration, testicle massage during doggystyle… – and, if he'd been with the woman for longer than one night, a list of predilections: counterclockwise cunnilingus, hair pulling (only during reverse cowgirl), light choking while blowing in ear and nibbling, light anal rimming (NO penetration).

The responses he got ranged from the expectedly hostile, threats of beatdowns and legal actions, to blocked profiles and email warnings from automated moderators, to nothing, a pregnant and wondering dead space.

Convincing himself that his work was vital, Eric had to persevere.

Which at first seemed kind of funny to her in a pitiful, if slightly messed up way. Then he started talking about the videos he made after enlisting the help of an IT guy from work with a penchant for tube sites. How they would download and combine clips from multiple scenes to create accurate depictions of the acts he'd described. How they would superimpose his head and the heads of the women he'd been with over the actors'. How it still didn't feel like enough. How he started making split-screen videos, juxtaposing the porn with images of himself performing weird approximations of the activities his former partners had enjoyed: attempting Bikram postures while naked, smearing on eyeliner and lip gloss and smiling into an off-camera mirror while adjusting a wig, lightly sliding a box cutter across his femoral artery while sobbing, his upper lip crusting and caked with blood and dust.

How the legal actions were no longer just threats.

She decides that the sun is worth it, leans back and stares at the tops of the trees beyond the garden sloping down the hill in front of them towards the stream until they vaporize along with her retinas and nothing hurts.

Eric's eyes roll back and it looks like he's about to try to channel some kind of epileptic white-boy voodoo: "I can't go, I can't go, I can't go to prison."

"You got nothing to worry about," Dave says. "You're prep-school soft."

Eric fiddles with the top button of his cardigan until it twists off in his hand. "Meaning what?"

"Meaning the closest you're ever going to get to real prison was when you got tripped up during a lacrosse game and someone's stick grazed your ass crack. Even if your pop's lawyer fucks up, you'll be on some white-collar Martha Stewart minimum-security shit, picking vegetables like we're doing here."

"My mother let my stepfather drive me to soccer tournaments until I was 12. He told me to pretend my foreskin was a Push Pop."

"There you go, already got in some bitch practice. Also, uhh?"

"No more lawyers. The apology payments stopped when I came here. If this place works it works;

194

maybe I change my name, get a retail job in a bedroom community in an outdoorsy state with a Mediterranean climate and a low rate of binge drinking and preventable hospitalizations. If it doesn't, I'm alone again, really alone. Cock-bait."

"Damn."

"Yeah."

"OK plan B then."

"Which is?"

"Death and destruction," she says.

"Ha! Blam! Don't give him any ideas baby girl. This dude's liable to take the next bus to the nearest middle school or movie theater and tear shit up!" Dave offers her a fist-bump, she accepts. "Actually I never really even had a Plan A. I just wanted to say 'Plan B' in a sentence that isn't related to me being woken up by some ratchet-ass trick whining about how I need to take her to the clinic. Ha! Right?"

She declines a second bump.

"Nah," Dave says, "but I still think the key is to find a sane chick willing to take care of you, to make you stop obsessing and cutting and whatever other weird shit you were doing. Maybe focus on what you want to look for when you get out of here, instead of feeling sorry for yourself and like moping and twitching all the time. Who do you want to be with and who do you want to be?"

"I've never really considered that," Eric says. "I always just thought I would meet a girl and just know it was right, you know? That they would cure me and everything would be different. I would become like them. I never thought about being, um, proactive and having a list of requirements, or like ever considered what was important to me and finding a partner who shared that. God, I've been doing it wrong the entire time, I'm such a –"

"We already know you're a dumbass bro. But now it's time for some, what do the counselors call it, inner retraction?"

"Inner reflection," she says.

"Right."

"I want someone who smells good when they smell bad," Eric says. "Who jogs regularly but doesn't care if I don't. Who hasn't totally given up on monogamy and the belief that a serious relationship is a foundation of mental and physical well-being. Who's kind of a feminist but doesn't want to completely tear down the current power structures or subvert gender roles. Who wears ironically hot librarian glasses to correct any vision problems à la Michelle Pfeiffer in Batman Returns. Who won't allow me to check out of the world completely but won't be aggressive, demanding, or unrealistic about reeling me back in, and won't compromise my masculinity in the process. Who realizes that I might be awkward and dysfunctional in bars and other similar social settings and knows that I'm only ignoring her sometimes because I never spent that much time with girls as a teenager and instead retreated into porn, chemical abuse, and multi-player online role-playing games. Who likes to cuddle even when I'm crying. Who doesn't have any dietary restrictions and isn't indecisive about where to eat on date nights. Who will be supportive of my recovery and won't make hostile or debilitating comments about my weight fluctuations. Who won't mistake sexual interest (and sexts) for misogyny. Who doesn't freak out because I'm sometimes clumsy, but always well-intentioned. Who changes her hair style three or four times a week to reflect her mood and outfit choices. Who never asks me if she can pull off bangs. Who doesn't see a prescription-induced lack of sex drive as overly problematic. Who won't ask to meet my mother. Who won't talk about my mother. Who wants to be with a mostly normal guy who's sick of being accused of horrible stuff and who understands that victimhood isn't a psychiatric disorder. Who likes 90s indie rock – think Pavement, Silver Jews, Toad the Wet Sprocket – and some retroactively catchy power-pop."

Dave's gut expands with choked-back laughter that tries to burst through the lining of his gray hoodie. "Bro I meant do you like blondes or brunettes, big tits or fat asses, Asians or Dominicans, not some crazy list of your mommy and step-daddy issues."

"I was reflecting," Eric says.

"You're still making everything about you. The woman is what you need, yes, but she's only a piece, like a stabilizer, nothing more. You've got to do the work to get better on your own. Man up. That's why people your age are fucked: you never get over yourselves and the kind-of-bad stuff that's happened to you. I see that shit already in some of my older kids."

"My age?" Eric mumbles, running his fingers across a purple-blotched cheek.

"Whining about people talking shit about them digitally, whatever. Why do you think you're single and perpetually screwed up? I'm like yo, have some real shit happen to you and then come back to me. Then we can talk."

Eric fidgets in his cardigan pockets, finds a loose pill in one of them, swallows it. He bows his head until his face is a few inches above the table, his breaths dispersing a few prematurely fallen seed pods.

"Have you sufficiently dealt with real shit?" she asks.

"From day one baby girl," Dave says. "The only time I can remember my pops laughing before he bounced out on us was when I was six and it was Thanksgiving and my mom told me to get napkins at the bodega. How the fuck was I supposed to know what 'sanitary napkins' were? When I brought them back and she started slapping me around for being a smartass, I heard this weird wheezing coming from across the room. Here's pops, this rotted-out, 250-pound lump of a former longshoreman and he's holding the pink box of pads, tears coming out of his eyes, his face turning all sorts of magenta, what it sounded like when he'd try to start his crusted Oldsmobile. That noise was scarier than anything they could ever do to me. Started playing in punk bands at 14, when punk wasn't some Green Day sing-along MTV swill, though I know that's hard for you to fathom. Got deep into the scene and involved with some real grimy gutter bitches, knocked up three that I know of, two that kept them. Stop me if you know where this is going."

"It's fine," she says, watching dusk overtake the garden. Dollops of drool puddle under Eric's nose.

"So then, duh, I got into standard strung-out asshole stuff, real stupid and high, stealing shit, did two years of a three-year bid for possession, went cold turkey while I was inside. Which was horrible, but not as bad as a few years later, after I'd been back on my feet, producing records for some bands you may have actually heard of, married, couple more kids, keeping my shit mostly together, until my flaming cunt of an ex decides this guy she sees at happy hour sometimes, this fat fucking claims adjuster from Long Island, is going to provide more of a 'stable environment' for her and my kids. Ha! This bitch is a Klonopin Pez dispenser, unstable enough for all of us. She should be the one here. I was locked up for seven hundred and sixteen days and didn't get anally raped until the first meeting with her divorce lawyer."

"Am I fat?" Eric whispers to the table, eyes clouded and dripping.

"You sneak Double Stuf Oreos after every meal and curl up in your room sobbing and touching yourself when we're supposed to being doing Pilates or rock climbing," Dave says. "Do you really want me to answer that? What I'm trying to say, baby girl and salivating moron, is that you define yourself by how good you are at forgetting. Not just the bad shit that's happened, the good shit you didn't do, the self-fulfilling screw-ups, the addiction. Forget about a future of finger-fucking princess charming, living a TV ending, collecting social security. The best chance you got is to look ahead, tunnel-vision, be smart enough to separate the good shit people do and say from the bad shit people do and say but not get too attached to either. Because you have to be in control when that fucked-up tide in the back of your head the counselors talk about starts to roll in. You know how hard it is to focus on holding it back; nobody but you can help with that. I'm cool with it. I'm good. Blam!"

"Then why are you here?" she says.

"Because my lady's old man used to manage a hedge fund and I occasionally drink too much wine when she has douchey friends over for dinner. More than occasionally. Not a good look, according to her. And, according to her, an end to her paying my child support and providing me with the kind of uppity lifestyle I've become accustomed to unless I complete a successful three-month vacation. Because maybe we're in love. And maybe the older you get, the more you realize love is really just a series of increasingly shitty and uncomfortable transactions with a payoff that shrinks faster than you do. Ha! Write that in your dark-ass notebook."

The sky bubbles rouge, a final breath, as the garden and patio gray into chalky monochrome. She feels a dew-mist begin to settle around them as the lights go on in the clinic's adjacent main building and the staff bungalows across the stream.

"Am I fat?" Eric says, looking up. "Like, be honest."

Dave looks at her, raises an eyebrow, waits for her permission to deliver a final punchline, a fatal blow.

She grins wide at neither of them, says, "We're all fucked," gets up and heads toward the main building and her room and a landline that, for the first time, she hopes won't ring.

*

Her dark hair is gathered up at the back of her head in a sloppy bun held together by a ballpoint pen, wavy strands framing her round cheeks. She pulls the pen, the one she's been using to sign the piles of wavers and confidentiality bullshit that will probably be incinerated once they let her leave, and shakes, letting the strands envelop her neck and shoulders.

A shroud rippling in the stream's reflection.

She lets out an unspoiled laugh at the grim image, one the counselors would call "delimiting" or "problematic," but she knows that darkness is transient, as much a part of herself as the thick eyelashes and eyes that flicker from brown and green to gray with the inconsistency of clouds.

It doesn't matter.

She presses on the space between her eyebrows and then her cheeks, waiting for the blush that isn't chemically regulated.

For a second she wishes the Ex or the bartender or anyone from school could see her like this, the way the flesh has spread and reclaimed itself, but she catches the thought and snuffs it like she's been training herself to do.

She opens her fists, closes. She unfurls the paper bag she's brought with her, empties its contents on the dock: a set of identical keys, the pills she's been hiding under her tongue and spitting for weeks, a gold nose ring.

Scooped into the water, she watches them drift, washed out of sight.

A tree-muffled conversation is coming towards her from somewhere back up the trail. Maybe it's her parents, uncharacteristically early to pick her up. She visualizes her father asking one of the counselors if the stream has any especially good fly fishing holes; her mother a few paces behind, nature-dazed and wary. Or it's Greta, her neighbor from down the hall who may have been prominently featured in several Nerf commercials two decades ago, and whose practice conversations with her PR team (using her Naltrexone bottle as a speaker phone) usually end with a monologue about outgrowing her regional territory, that she's "L.A.-ready."

Or, nothing. The departure of echoes from a scrubbed-out space.

She slides into the water.

She pulls her tee shirt over her head and lets it glide away, frees one leg then the other from the muck-slick bottom. She allows herself to merge with the current and extends her arms to stabilize the pace, not reaching for something to hold.

The Terrible Softness

How has it come to this, he would think, zoning on the pixels that flickered, MRI-slow, from the screen on his blanket-covered stomach. Regardless of how hard I try, I can't seem to keep my shit together.

Fundamentally, he knew you couldn't keep any kind of shit together. Everything was carbon and particles smaller than carbon and those particles were always corroding, breaking, collapsing against each other with the terrible softness of tongues. A rapid, infinite sequence of shifts that didn't stop and were at once fragile and impenetrably brutal. If he felt a pang of irrational strength, he would try to fight the changes: he would dismantle his power cord, close the screen, his thoughts, his head, and for as long as he could, forget the events, faces, and hips that had come to define his particular disintegration.

He would stay in one place and keep staying still. He would hold his breath and try not to desire it.

Simply absorb fluids.

Keep your shit together.

He could still feel the dense and desperate oscillations, though muffled, continuing unabated, buzzing in directions he wasn't even aware of, reminders of his task's impossibility.

He would open his laptop and jerk off and sometimes sleep soundly.

One night during a routine meandering, he watched a clip of a husband/wife team of amateur bow-hunting enthusiasts with a moderately large subscriber base. He knew the video was recent because of the date it was posted and because the foliage in the background was as barren as the few trees in his neighborhood at an almost equivalent latitude.

He assumed from the comments section that the wife had shot the large antlered mammal the pair was crouching over, then groping – "NICE buck hunnie!!! love that you guys got the whole family in on that its amazing! cant wait to get some meat in the fridge :)." A pink-shafted arrow protruded from the base of the animal's neck. Its hide was covered in mud and fallen leaves from the ground where it had whined and twisted.

Where once it had eaten and fucked and shat and now died.

The video ended and he placed his laptop on the floor next to his bed.

He didn't think about how the husband and wife had concluded by taking a selfie and making out while straddling the carcass. How Dana, if she hadn't moved out last week, would probably have cried and wanted to hold the animal in her too-brittle arms. How the animal hadn't done anything that animals shouldn't do.

He fixated on the decaying plant matter licking the animal and the ground, returning everything around it to a place beyond change.

Now that the leaves are almost gone, he thought, maybe I'll be able to keep my shit together.

One day soon, when all the leaves are gone.